A FIGURE IN GREY

By the same author

FELIX WALKING

FELIX RUNNING

Published by Eyre Methuen

BELLA ON THE ROOF

Published by Longmans Green

A FIGURE IN GREY

HILARY
FORD

WORLD'S WORK LTD

Published by
World's Work Ltd.
The Windmill Press
Kingswood, Tadworth, Surrey.

SBN 437 40350 5

Printed in Great Britain by
Cox & Wyman, Ltd.
London, Fakenham and Reading

I

The kitchen, Katharine saw as she came in through the back door, was in a worse state than usual. There were dishes piled high in the sink, the floor was grubby with scraps of food and milk spilled from the cat's bowl, and the uncleared table was scattered with cake crumbs. It also held a plate smeared with peanut butter, a half-empty glass of orange squash beside the almost empty bottle of concentrate, and slightly less than half a chain-store chocolate cake. Plus a loaf spilling slices from its wrapper, a butter dish with the lid upside down beside it, and the jar of peanut butter on its side with the top missing.

She went grim-faced in search of Sarah. She pushed open the front-door with no more than a quick peremptory knock, expecting to catch a scuffling movement as a book was concealed. But Sarah was genuinely doing prep, pen laboriously moving across the page of an exercise book. She looked up and innocently said hello.

"The kitchen," Katharine said.

"What about it?"

"It's a pigsty."

"It was like that when I came in."

"The table wasn't."

"Well, there didn't seem any point . . ."

5

"Come and do it. Now."

"But, Kate, I've got an essay for Miss Pedersen and a double lot of arithmetic and . . ."

"Now."

She came, sighing heavily, and went on sighing heavily as she sorted out the clutter on the table. Katharine was sweeping the floor; it really, she thought, needed scrubbing. She said,

"And did you have to eat more than half the chocolate cake? And that bottle of orange squash was new yesterday. You're a pig, Sarah."

She spoke with cold anger. Sarah drew an even gustier sigh and did not answer. After a moment or two she said,

"I'll go and get on with my prep."

Katharine straightened up. "Oh no, you won't! There's the sink to clear."

"But *I* didn't leave it."

"Makes no difference."

"And it's Gwen's day for duty."

"You know she's at St John's."

"I don't see why that means I've got to do it."

"I'm doing it as well."

"And I've got so much prep tonight. Miss Pedersen said we've to hand in at least four pages."

"Do you imagine I've not got any? You haven't even wiped the table properly."

Sarah took a cloth and made an ineffectual sweeping movement. She sighed again. She *ought* to be made do her share, Katharine thought, but resentment over her younger sister's talent for getting away with things was balanced by irritation at having her around. And it might be true about the prep. She said sharply,

"Go on then. But if I come in and find you reading . . ."

6

Katharine had just finished the dishes and cleaned the sink when her mother got back. She said,

"Oh, Kate, have you done all that yourself? I am terrible. I was just going to get started when Ann Gamble rang, and I couldn't get her off the telephone. And then it was time to go out to this wretched meeting and I had to leave everything. Darling, can you pop the kettle on? I'm beat, absolutely beat."

Katharine's mother was a small thin woman with a mop of dark unruly hair and big eyes. She had never been pretty but people always said she had a fascinating personality. She gave Katharine a quick hug and went through the kitchen and upstairs. Katharine had tea ready when she came down, five minutes later. Her mother said,

"And I think I'll have a chocolate biscuit if you'd be a darling and get them for me. Have you had some tea?"

Katharine shook her head. "I didn't want any."

"But you should. You're much too young to go in for that stupid slimming."

Katharine said untruthfully, "It's nothing to do with slimming."

"You're the only one who does it."

"Sarah *ought* to. Half a chocolate cake again, and she almost finished the bottle of orange. Mother, you ought to do something about it."

"She does love eating. So does Gwen."

"Gwen can get away with it." That was said with a touch of bitterness. "Sarah can't."

"You take things a bit too seriously at times. A little puppy fat is natural in a girl. She'll grow out of it."

"I don't think she will. And she was crying at school yesterday. Somone called her 'Fatso'."

"Well, if she cares about it she'll stop overeating."

"No, she won't."

7

"If she cares enough. Kate, you're frowning. You must stop worrying so much about everything." She looked at her daughter critically. "You know, really you ought to be the prettiest of the three. You've got the best bone structure. It's your expression that lets you down. Either shy and a bit sullen, or worrying. You need to be more lighthearted. Aren't you having a cup of tea, even?"

"No. I ought to be getting down to my prep. There's quite a load."

"Not just yet. I want to tell you about the meeting. An absolutely terrible case we had. These two children . . ."

It really was terrible. Her mother filled in the harrowing details of a case of neglect, mother having gone off and father almost permanently drunk. Katharine listened reluctantly. She did not like herself for her reluctance, but it always upset her to be told of horrors which she could do nothing to help. That was a wrong attitude, though. And the Society was doing something; her mother was helping. The children were being taken into care. Katharine had a brief vision of what *that* might be like, of the strangeness, unfamiliar surroundings, not knowing what was happening or going to happen . . .

Her mother looked round the now fairly tidy kitchen with approval. She said,

"It's awful to realize what some little ones have to go through. You ought to think about it, Kate."

"Yes," Katharine said, "I know. I'd really better get some work done."

"Just a minute." Her mother took another chocolate biscuit. Like Gwen she could eat anything without putting on an ounce. "I've got something to tell you. A surprise."

"Yes?"

"About the summer holidays. Aunt Marion's asked you to go to her."

8

Katharine was staggered. "Asked me?"

"All of you. For a month in August."

"But why?"

"It's an idea of hers. A very kind thought."

"She's never done before."

"It's a kind thought all the same."

It was difficult to take in. Aunt Marion as a feature in their lives was fixed, predictable and infrequent. A letter at Christmas with presents: small cheap ones, usually unattractive. Similar presents and cards on birthdays. And once a year the ceremonious visit when she came to London to see her lawyer and her broker. She stayed two nights in a gloomy hotel in Bloomsbury which had a conservatory full of sinister dark green, oily-looking plants. It was always during the Easter holidays and she always, on the afternoon of the second day, took the Morris girls to a theatre matinee. Her most recent visit had been a month earlier and she had taken them to "The Mousetrap", despite having previously taken them to it four years before. She had not then, or at any time, made any suggestion about their visiting her at her home near Manpool.

Katharine said, "But I don't understand. Why – after all this time?"

"She's getting old."

That was true. She was about sixty-five, Katharine supposed, but looked older. She wore long heavy silk dresses, dark blue or green or brown – dark at any rate. From the last encounter Katharine recalled a triple rope of pearls that seemed too big and white to be real, a big gold cameo brooch, and a gold pin with a red stone in the end that kept her hat in place on top of her coiled grey hair. Her manner was awkward, her voice low and thin and difficult to follow. She either sat in silence or asked

9

stupid questions, chiefly about school and how they were getting on there. She was simply tedious, a bore.

Katharine said, "Do we have to go? We don't, do we?"

"It's a marvellous opportunity for you. She's got a wonderful house. Your father and I visited her once, not long after we were married."

"But in Manpool . . ."

Her mother had always been outspokenly contemptuous of the North, particularly the industrial North. There was a saying she trotted out from time to time – "Hell begins north of a line drawn between Cardiff and the Wash." It usually raised a laugh. Manpool, by that standard, was well inside the infernal region, a grubby, smoky seaport of which she had never heard any good.

"It's on the outskirts and it's in its own grounds – acres and acres of them. You'd never know you were near a city."

"What about Devon?" Katharine asked.

Their usual holiday centred round a cottage they rented for a fortnight, not far from Ilfracombe. They had done so for as long as Katharine could remember. Her mother said,

"This will be much better for you. Twice as long." She went on quickly, "I'm not sure we could have managed Devon this year, anyway. They were putting the rent of the cottage up – almost double."

"Couldn't we just stay at home in that case?"

"Katharine," her mother said with irritation, "I don't understand why you're being so difficult about this. If she *had* just asked you by yourself – I know there's that unfortunate shyness of yours – but there will be the three of you. You must try to get out of the habit of clinging to routines; it's awful in someone as young as you are."

She looked at her watch.

"Oh, Lord, I was supposed to ring Hetty Cambridge. Darling, didn't you say you had a lot of prep to do?"

Katherine told the others later, after Gwen had got back from her St John's Ambulance training class. Sarah took it in silent dismay with a hint of brimming eyes; she cried easily. Gwen said dramatically,

"You can't mean it! A month with Aunt Marion – I couldn't bear it. I'd be stark screaming mad inside two days. Didn't you tell Mother it was impossible?"

"I tried. She wasn't listening."

"We'll all tell her. She can't *make* us go."

Katharine said, "You know how enthusiastic she gets about things. We'll need to give her time to cool down a bit."

Gwen said, "We must go to Devon. I've told Robin we're going."

Robin was her current boy friend. Katharine, who had no boy friend and was almost sure she despised the notion of having one, said sarcastically,

"I don't quite see what that's got to do with anything."

"Because he's got a plan, imbecile. To join us. He's just about got his parents to agree to him going on a cycling holiday with Dennis Ryder. They're taking their bikes down there by train. We can't not go."

"Oh, really?" Katharine said. "Who cares about Robin Red Spot?" That was an unkind reference to the acne which plagued him: Gwen punched viciously but from long practice Katharine rode the blow. "Never mind. We can't do anything right away. I'll talk to Daddy later on."

"We all will."

"If we do he'll back up Mother. He's bound to."

Gwen recognized the truth of this. She said,

"As long as you make it absolutely clear the whole idea is quite *impossible*."

"Would you rather handle it?"

"No, I suppose not. You're better at that sort of thing. More devious." Gwen stretched out a black-nyloned leg and said bitterly, "Look, another ladder. And Mother says I can't have any more stockings till next month. I'll have to go on parade with this." She looked at the world with angry eyes. "It's just not fair."

It was a fine evening and after supper Mr Morris went out into the garden. This was not large, a rectangle of fifty feet by less than twenty like all the others behind the row of semi-detached houses, but he spent a lot of time in it. As Katharine approached he was stooping over an azalea bush which seemed, now in the middle of its brief season of blossoming, almost on fire against the drooping dusk. He straightened up, a tall thin man with a lumpy face and a bald patch on his head. He taught geography and history, not in the big gleaming comprehensive school to which Katharine and her sisters went, but in a rundown boys' secondary modern a mile away.

"Not bad for a London suburb." He pointed to the azalea. "Considering she hails originally from the Asian mountains. Some immigrants do better than others in alien soil."

Katharine said: "Daddy, about going to Aunt Marion in summer – we don't have to, do we?"

He looked at her. "Don't you want to?"

"We'd rather go to Devon."

"Well, there are some difficulties about that."

"The rent going up? Mother said. But we could economize in other ways. We needn't have trips into

Ilfracombe or Barnstaple. They cost quite a bit. We could stay around the cottage and save money."

"There's more to it."

"What?"

"Your aunt has asked you to stay. Bit rude to say you won't come."

"But not for a month! We could go for a week-end, and still go to Devon."

"She's asked you for a month."

"But she's never bothered before. It's just some silly whim she's got in her head."

"She's an old lady. You have to humour her."

"Not to the extent of letting her ruin our holiday, surely? Couldn't you say you'd already made arrangements and it was too late to change? It's only a couple of months off, after all."

"She had a heart attack just after Christmas."

"You're not saying our refusing to let her boss us might give her another, and kill her?"

"No, not exactly." He was smiling but not at ease. "You don't know much about your aunt, do you?"

"We see her every year." Katharine thought about it. "No, I don't suppose we do. Not much."

"She's a very wealthy woman."

"Is she? That's a tatty hotel she stays in. And she's pretty mean with her presents. She sent me an initialled handkerchief for my last birthday."

"Rich people often are a bit mean in small things. Actually she isn't really your aunt, of course; she's your first cousin, twice removed. I think that's the size of it, anyway: your grandmother and she were cousins.

"Your great-great-grandfather had half a dozen daughters but only two grew up and got married. The elder was reckoned to be the prettier, but it was the younger who married well – a man who had money and made a lot more, in shipping. There was probably some resentment on the other side. At any rate the two branches drifted apart. Even without bad feeling that can happen very easily when one lot has money and the other hasn't."

He was in one of his rambling moods, Katharine thought impatiently. She said:

"Yes, I suppose it can."

"She's kept in touch with us," her father said, "– as a duty, I suppose. But she's always made it clear that there was nothing to be expected from her. Everything was to go to her nephew, her brother's son in Rhodesia. Now it seems she's fallen out with him."

Suddenly she took the point. "You mean, she might leave *us* something?"

"It's possible. She really is very rich."

"Well, she can can keep it. We don't want her money."

"Don't we?"

"No. Surely not."

"I approve the sentiment, but it's not as simple as all that. I'm a poor schoolmaster." Katharine cringed and did her best to cover her embarrassment. "Expenses are high and they keep getting higher. I've got at least one daughter who's university material. That prospect's not so far off."

Katharine had been top in her form three terms running. She said:

"If I get a place I'll get a grant as well."

"Yes, but it would be nice to think there was a little extra."

"I'd rather . . ."

"Not to mention Gwen and Sarah. Whether or not they go to university they'll need training, expensive training, if they're to have decent careers."

14

The importance of decent careers for girls was one of their mother's favourite topics. Katharine argued:

"But we can manage – we would have done. Much better than hoping Aunt Marion is going to leave us something. She'll probably live till a hundred, anyway."

She paused as the real significance of the holiday business finally got home to her: they were to go and stay with Aunt Marion and be nice to her for the sake of her money . . . She said:

"We couldn't! Suck up to her, you mean?"

"I didn't say that." He was indignant but also, she thought, a little guilty. "It's the last thing we'd want you to do. Being polite to an old lady who takes an interest in you is not the same as toadying."

She could have argued that and would have done, but something else occurred to her.

"Anyway, what about you and Mother? If we go to Aunt Marion instead of Devon, you won't have a holiday at all."

He walked towards the tool shed and Katharine followed him.

"That's another thing, Kate. It's been a long time since your mother had a proper holiday. Even in Devon there's the cottage to look after – cleaning, cooking and all that."

She was hurt that he had not apparently noticed how much of the all that had in fact been done by her, but only said:

"We could do everything. I'll make the girls lend a hand."

"The point is, if we knew you were safe and sound with Aunt Marion I might take her somewhere nice, abroad perhaps. I know she'd like to see France again. We haven't been there since you were born."

Katharine said: "Yes." It took the wind out of her sails. "Of course."

"You understand, don't you?"

"Yes." She could have argued the money thing, but not this. "It's a super idea."

He squeezed her shoulder and she managed not to flinch away. "I can rely on you to put it over to the others?"

"Yes. Yes, of course."

"Good old Kate. You know, you'll find you do have a good time. A big rambling house, tremendous grounds – plenty to explore."

"Yes," she said for what seemed the hundredth time.

The following Saturday evening, about nine-thirty, Katharine heard the front door slam in a familiar fashion, followed by the sound of feet thumping heavily up the stairs. The door of the bedroom she shared with Gwen was pushed open and Gwen, without greeting, went to her bed and flung herself down on it. Katharine thought of saying something, in particular something sharp about people who entered rooms without knocking – a crime Gwen was always condemning in Sarah – but decided it was not worth precipitating the storm. It was probably about due to burst, anyway.

Silence hung like a suffocating cloud for several minutes. In the end, Katharine said,

"For goodness' sake, Gwen, what's the gloom about?"

"Damn," Gwen said. "Damn, damn, damn, damn! Damn everything."

"What in particular?" Katharine asked. "Or who?"

Gwen had gone out after supper in ebullient mood. She was meeting Robin at a coffee-bar called the Hive, which was where their particular gang gathered at the moment. It had honey-coloured walls and mobiles of bees drifting round and something that made a gentle background buzzing noise in the rare intervals when the jukebox was not playing. Table tops were printed with psychedelic petals and the backs of the booths with hollyhocks, delphiniums and similar rather showy flowers. Katharine had been there a couple of times and did not like it.

"Robin," Gwen said, "the cretinous ape."

It would be unwise, Katharine thought, to agree openly. She waited, and after a few moments the explanation burst out.

He had been late for a start, nearly ten minutes, with some feeble excuse about having been made to clean his bicycle. On a Saturday evening! Then he had slopped coffee in the saucer when he brought their drinks, and suggested she pour it back in the cup when she pointed this out to him. Then when she had told him her scheme . . .

"What scheme?" Katharine asked.

Gwen said impatiently. "That they should switch to Manpool as well, of course. They could take their bikes there by train as easily as Barnstaple."

"Ah," Katharine said. "It was no go?"

" 'I'm not sure we could do that.' "

She mimicked Robin's cautious and in Katharine's view decidedly wet voice quite well.

"Any particular reason?"

"That's what I asked him. He said because of Dennis. So I asked him *why* because of Dennis. He said he didn't think Dennis would want to go up north, and besides he was keen on Ilfracombe because he knew someone down there who had a boat and they might get some sailing."

"The urge to the sea," Katharine said. "Not surprising. He looks fishy."

Gwen giggled. Dennis was a lank awkward boy with a long lugubrious face that had a peculiar damp look. Remembering her indignation, she said,

"I asked him if he had to do everything Dennis wanted, didn't he have a mind of his own? Then he went on about his parents only agreeing to the cycling holiday because of Dennis. His mother thinks Dennis is very reliable. Reliable . . .!"

"So no luck?" Katharine said.

"He said something vague about talking it over with Dennis, but he was obviously just saying that. So I told him what I thought of him and walked out."

"Just what?" Katharine asked with interest.

"I told him he was a weak-kneed pointless drip and that he'd better go and find his sweaty friend and start planning their sailing. Though I said a paddle-boat in the lake at Battersea Park Funfair was about their level really. I told him I was fed up with his grotty voice anyway, and his habit of sniffing all the time, and that he wouldn't have so many pimples if he washed his face properly."

"Well, well," Katharine said. "I take it the romance is over?"

"Romance!"

Gwen flung herself back on the bed. She wept violently and, between sobs, said what she thought of Aunt Marion and her comic schemes for holidays. When there was an interval into which a few words might be slid, Katharine said,

"It's probably worked out for the best, though, hasn't it?"

Gwen stared at her, face blotched. "It's all right for you! You don't have any feelings, deep feelings anyway."

"But if you've realized he's a drip . . ."

"I can't *stand* him!"

"Better now, surely, than later."

"Oh, you don't understand!"

Katherine felt she did have a glimmering. A boy she couldn't stand was, as far as Gwen was concerned, much less of a calamity than no boy at all. And she had been looking forward to having two of them in Devon, with the delicious possibilities of playing one off against the other. However unsatisfactory and unattractive they might be in person, the prospect was not one she could willingly contemplate giving up.

The sobbing continued, if anything growing heavier. The good thing about Gwen's storms was that the more violent they were the sooner they were over.

Sarah's crisis came a few days later. She had been in the bathroom a long time, washing her hair, and there had been some altercation between her and Gwen, and banging on the door from the latter. When Sarah finally emerged she told Gwen the bathroom was free. Gwen said angrily,

"About time! Honestly, the way you drag everything out . . ."

Sarah said, "Oh, stop being a misery! You've been like this ever since we were told about the holiday. It's the same for all of us. You're making things worse by keeping on about it. It won't be as bad as all that."

"Listen to Sunny Sal!"

"That's true, Kate, isn't it?"

"Just wait and see," Gwen said. "You say that because you haven't thought about it. One little item: miles of woods all round. No shop on the corner where you can buy bars of chocolate to hide under your pillow."

The chocolate episode was one in which Sarah had been

caught at the beginning of term. She flushed and said defiantly,

"I don't care about that."

"No public library, either."

She was hitting hard. Sarah turned away and started to leave the room. Gwen called after her,

"And no Garance to smuggle into your bed at night. No Garance for a month."

Garance, the Siamese cat, was theoretically a family animal but reserved ninety per cent at least of her weird affection for Sarah. Sarah's head came round sharply.

"We can take her with us. We took her down to Devon."

Where, after a morning's yowling, she had settled down with perfect self-possession, treating the rolling hillside on which the cottage stood with the same authority and air of command that she did the Borough of Wandsworth.

"Not to Aunt Marion's, though," Gwen said.

Sarah looked in appeal to Katharine.

"We can, can't we?"

Katharine shook her head. "I'm afraid not."

"But we must!" Her face cleared slightly. "We'll have to. Mother and Daddy – they won't be here to look after her, and they can't take her to France with them. She would have to go into quarantine when she came back and it lasts for ever."

Katharine said, "Mother's arranging for her to be boarded, in a cat home."

Sarah wailed, "But she can't! Not Garance . . . She'd absolutely hate it. She'd pine. She might die!"

Katharine said, "Don't be silly. Of course she won't die. She'll be very well looked after."

Sarah stood by the door, tears rolling down her cheeks. Mimicking her earlier remark, Gwen said, "Oh, stop being a misery!"

"And you stop tormenting her, for goodness' sake," Katharine said with irritation. "Things are bad enough without that."

That night Katharine lay awake for some time, staring at a patch of moonlight on the wall. From Gwen's bed came the sound of deep and even breathing. Her emotional storms, however dramatic, never kept her from sleeping.

Sarah would get over being without Garance after a couple of days, and Gwen's miseries were not long-lived. Altogether things might not be too bad. If you *had* to do something the sensible thing was to look on the bright side. A rambling house, her father had said, and plenty to explore in the grounds. They might not have to see too much of Aunt Marion. When they did, of course, they must do their best to be nice to her.

Picturing this, her own dread came to the surface. She remembered also what her father had said about Aunt Marion's money. Being nice was something which could easily be regarded in a different light. The viewpoint shifted so that she was not merely visualizing Aunt Marion but also reading her thoughts, seeing politeness as wheedling, smiles as the tricks of shameless beggars. Her flesh crawled with humiliation.

2

The station at Manpool was much the same as the main London stations in size and general appearance and yet it seemed different. Something to do with the people on the platforms, Katharine thought. It was not anything one could put a finger on. The way they moved, perhaps. Faster, or slower? Differently, anyway. She told herself it was ridiculous; there only seemed a difference because she was expecting it. They reached the ticket barrier and she produced the tickets and concentrated on looking for Aunt Marion's chauffeur.

He was standing on the right, just beyond the barrier. They could scarcely have missed him because apart from being in the place Aunt Marion's letter had indicated, he was wearing the black uniform she had mentioned with the high peaked cap. He was also a couple of inches over six feet. In addition he made straight for them with a purposeful look.

"The Misses Morris," he said, "– that right? Captain Benger, at your service. Where's all the bags, then?"

He had a strange voice, high and throaty, the accent north-country but with the vowel sounds modified as if he were making an attempt to talk BBC. A half-hearted attempt, though, and one of which he appeared to be unconscious.

Katharine said, "Over there. That porter . . ."

"Righty-o. I'll see to things."

He sharply directed the porter to follow and led the way across the station hall. The pace was brisk and Sarah almost had to run to keep up. He noticed that, and slowed down. Sarah said, breathing in deeply,

"I can smell the sea."

Her senses were keener than the others. Katharine sniffed the air herself and was not sure whether she could pick up the tang of salt or not. The Captain said approvingly,

"Right enough. Not more than a couple of hundred yards down the hill." He made a lot of the aitches. "You used to be able to see it when you came out into George Street, but that was before the war. They built up higher after the blitz. There was a real smell to George Street station in those days. The wind came up Bannister Street, right off the sea, full of brine, and mixed with the smell of the trains, coal-fired not these diesels. I used to think about that when I was out in Africa. Beat all your orange groves and pomegranates."

They came out of the station into the forecourt. On one side there was a taxi rank, on the other a row of parked cars, most of them large and gleaming. The Captain turned that way and Katharine wondered which their car would be. A Bentley looked as though it would go best with the smartly creased uniform and stiff peaked cap; but he went past it and the Jaguar which was her second choice. The car at which he stopped was large, too, but not magnificent. It was a black estate car, at least thirty years old, which had a wide running board at the side with a rubber surface worn through into holes. The seat covers were of old leather, cracked and shiny, mended in places with thick black thread.

Katharine had the two tenpenny pieces in her hand,

23

ready to tip the porter, but the Captain gave her no chance to approach him. He gave sharp and explicit instructions about stacking their luggage in the space at the back, forcing the porter to take Gwen's case out and put it in a different way, and then tipped him with a dismissive way. And with, Katharine noticed, a twopenny piece. The porter looked at the coin incredulously, looked at the Captain, started to say something, then shrugged in gloomy resignation and walked away. The Captain courteously saw them into the wide back seat, closed their door, and got into the driving-seat.

"Righty-o," he said. "Hold tight, and off we go."

The day was grey and windy, blowing scraps of paper along the pavements, but the city would have been depressing, Katharine thought, in any weather. She saw some shops that looked mildly interesting but the streets, after central London, seemed small and provincial. The buses were not red but green, and not even the deep familiar green of the Green Line coaches but a paler, more washed-out shade. The Captain drove in a stream of traffic that moved by stops and starts and the streets seemed to go on for ever, dingier now, the shops really dull by this time. Gwen, sitting on the far side with Sarah between them, made an expressive gesture of disgust and despair behind the Captain's back.

They passed through an even more depressing area with a number of very old-fashioned factories, tall-chimneyed, surrounded by high blank grimy walls. Gradually, after about half an hour, they emerged into suburbs, and the road was flanked by rows of semi-detached houses with tiny gardens. These, too, looked smaller and meaner than the ones she was used to, faced with ugly pebble dashing and for the most part needing painting.

The car, although the road was clearer, continued to

crawl. Katharine craned her neck and saw that the speedometer was registering twenty. Gwen, who had also glanced at it, said suddenly,

"Is this . . . ?"

She stopped. The Captain said,

"Is this what, miss?"

"As fast as the car will go?"

He gave a reproving wag of the head; his hair was cropped close and his face, apart from a short grey moustache, closely shaven. He was in his late fifties, thin-featured with a jaw that stuck out.

"Built to do over eighty, and she could do it still if required. I keep her in pretty good order."

They were passed by a small pre-Mini Austin, driven by a white-haired old lady. Gwen looked as though she were going to say something else, but Katharine's glance stopped her. The Captain went on,

"But she's a heavy drinker at anything over twenty-five, and Miss Hunston sees no sense in wasting petrol. I've heard her say: there aren't many things you need to hurry for, and for most of them you'll be late anyway."

He turned off the main road into the housing estate itself. Katharine had a sudden flash of thinking that perhaps the rambling house and the acres of grounds was a fantasy, that Aunt Marion lived in one of these houses with scuffed gardens and washing blowing on the lines at the back. Then she saw open space ahead, and a long high stone wall curving away. The houses ended and the road changed, showing potholes and cracks instead of smooth tarmac. Just past the last of the council houses there was a wooden post with a board above it. The board was white with black lettering. The paint had flaked badly but the message could just be read:

PRIVATE ROAD TO HUNSTON HOUSE
STRICTLY NO ADMITTANCE
EXCEPT ON BUSINESS.

The road went on for another fifty yards ending at a
point where the wall's blank grey expanse gave way to a
small square cottage, a lodge she supposed, and high
iron gates. The Captain nudged the car up close to these,
stopped it, and got out. He produced a large iron key and
put it in a lock in the right-hand gate. It squealed hideously
as he turned it.

Katharine looked about her. Between the wall and the
council houses there was a sort of no-man's-land of unkempt
grass. The wall itself, she now saw, apart from being
something like ten feet high, had its top studded with
nasty-looking bits of glass. The gates were of matching
height and one of them had another board wired to it.
The message this time said:

BEWARE SAVAGE DOGS

The lodge had two outward-facing windows, both
empty of glass, and looked like a ruin inside. The Captain
returned, drove the car through the gateway, and went
back to lock the gates behind him. On *this* side the lodge
windows were completely boarded up and a door had a
heavy bolt on the outside. Trespassers who came in
through the outer windows would not get very much
further.

Sarah asked, as the Captain returned, stowing the key
away in a trouser pocket,

"What kind of dogs are they?"

"Dogs?"

"The notice. Savage dogs."

He chuckled throatily. "That's a bit out-of-date, you

might say. Thirty years or more. But it helps keep the kids out." He laughed. "I've heard tales about packs of wolfhounds. People say they hear them howling at night."

"Doesn't Aunt Marion have any dogs now?" Sarah asked.

"Not even a Peke. Mrs Castle has a cat, but I wouldn't call it savage. Hasn't done anything but eat and sleep for the last five years."

The road continued as a drive. This, too, had at one time been tarmacadamed but was in even worse condition than the stretch outside. They really crept along, with the Captain obviously trying to steer round the potholes but not managing to miss them all. The car lurched and jolted, once throwing them all forward in a jumbled heap. Gwen, recalling a comment of their father, said,

"Bit hard on the springs, isn't it?"

"A bit," the Captain said. "But at least she can take it better than one of these modern tin cans would. Motors really did have springs when this was built. I remember being in this same model doing over sixty across the Western Desert."

"Western Desert?" Gwen asked.

"One of Monty's men," the Captain said. "Keeping a straight bat and knocking the Hun for six." He laughed in a high cackle. "All the way from Alamein to Algiers."

The car hit another rut and bounced out of it. Katharine said,

"Couldn't they be filled in – the holes?"

"Costs money," the Captain said. "And a fair amount on a road getting on for two miles long. A new set of springs would be cheaper."

"What about other people?"

"There aren't any. No tradesmen – we collect our own

stuff. And Miss Hunston isn't much given to visiting or being visited."

They had been travelling through a wood that pressed close on either side; not a disciplined orderly wood but one tangled and dark, overgrown with bushes. Quite suddenly these gave way to an open space which dipped ahead and to the right. It was a saucer of rough land, several hundred yards across – humped and hollowed, with a few thorn and gorse bushes, but otherwise mostly short grass and bracken. Katharine saw a bank full of rabbit holes exposing sandy earth within.

The house stood on the far side of the saucer, reached by the road which wound round the side to get to it. Looking at it for the first time, Katharine had a strange unsettling feeling: that it was a place she had not only seen before but knew very well. The very oddness of the structure made the feeling more convincing. The familiarity surely could not be due to confusing it with her memory of somewhere else; there could not have been another house much like this.

The chief impression it gave was of having been improvised by several different builders, working not only individually and in widely separated times but even in a spirit of mutual defiance. The part nearest to them was low lying, on two levels only, built in yellow stone streaked with grey and dotted with small windows that did not quite match. There were even lower outlying buildings tacked on at the back. The central part of the house, rising above the rest in superior fashion, was red-bricked in orthodox Georgian style and had a large front door with steps leading to it and columns holding up a fanlighted porch. The bit beyond was again lower and seemed to be built of glass. Last came the weirdest and most defiant contribution of all: a high round tower with a yellow base but with a red turreted battlement round the top.

"Goodness," Sarah said, "it's big."

"Right enough," the Captain said. He appeared to speak with feeling. "Too big for what Miss Hunston needs."

Gwen asked, "Is it very old?"

"Some parts are. That near bit is. Sixteenth century, or seventeenth. An old farmhouse originally – that was before the land was let go to timber, of course. Good Queen Bess very likely stayed there and milked a cow or two." He laughed. "Then the main bit was built on by some admiral or other who's supposed to have made a pile in prize money during the war against Napoleon. And Miss Hunston's father did the rest – the big conservatory first and then the tower. The conservatory was because he had some notion of growing his own oranges and bananas. Don't know if he ever managed it even with glass. I'm not sure what the tower was for. He was a bit eccentric, by all accounts.

Sarah said, "It does look old. Is it . . ."

"Is it what?"

"Haunted?"

"Do you believe in ghosts, then?"

"No." She was flushing. "No, I don't."

"So it can't be, can it?"

"What I meant . . . is it *supposed* to be haunted?"

"Not all that much. No more than two or three that I've heard of."

"But you haven't – seen any?"

"How could I," asked the Captain, "if there aren't none?"

"But . . ."

"Here we are," the Captain said. "Home at last, safe and sound."

He pulled the car up in front of the steps. These, like the porch, were less impressive at close quarters, showing cracks and a sag at one side. The pillars had apparently been painted red originally – traces of paint adhered to otherwise grey and weather-roughened surfaces. One of the panes in the fanlight was cracked across. The front door opened while they were getting out of the car and a figure appeared. Aunt Marion, Katharine thought, and then saw it was someone smaller and fatter. Presumably the Mrs Castle who had the cat.

Soaking in a bath that evening, Katharine tried to collect her impressions and make something coherent of them. The bathroom itself was extraordinary: bigger than their sitting-room at home, with a ceiling about twenty feet high and the various fixtures – bath, wash-basin, lavatory – separated from each other by yards of tiled floor. The tiles were lozenge-shaped, alternating black and white. The taps were of brass, badly tarnished, and enormous. The lavatory sat up on a little platform and had its bowl decorated with blue roses. The bath in which she was lying was very long and if she did not hang on to the brass rail fitted down one side she found herself floating away towards the taps at the end.

The head of the bath faced a large window, for the most part made up of small panes of stained glass – red and yellow squares at either side but in the middle a more ambitious work, a naval scene. Sailing ships were dotted about on a blue-green sea. It was a depiction of some battle, probably, because at least one ship seemed to be firing its cannons. Unfortunately in the centre a rectangle of clear glass had replaced a section that had presumably been broken, which made it difficult to work out just what was meant to be going on.

The clear bit was large enough to give one a view out, across the open land towards the woods. The grey blowy day had degenerated into a greyer dusk. Small specks of black swooped and darted. Not birds so late as this: bats, more likely. She wondered if they nested in the house – in the tower or one of the outbuildings – and felt a shiver of distaste.

But the distaste was fleeting; principally she felt at ease here and – it was the only term that fitted – at home. She thought again about her first reaction to seeing the house from a distance, the sense of familiarity. She had read about that sort of thing, though she had never experienced it. But there could be a simpler, more straightforward explanation. Her mother had said she and her father had stayed here once, not long after they were married. There might have been a view of it in that box of jumbled photographs which her father was always saying he was going to sort out and arrange some day. As a child she had sometimes browsed through them on wet afternoons, astonished by glimpses of her mother in a high-necked bathing costume, her father young and thin in khaki uniform. That was years ago, but she supposed the memory could have stayed somewhere at the back of her mind.

She looked up and saw a crack in the ceiling, whose plaster anyway was greyish and flaking. The house was ramshackle and not too clean. Mrs Castle was the house-keeper but apparently saw to everything without help: cooking and cleaning and looking after Aunt Marion. She was in her fifties, small, fattish, red-faced. She smoked incessantly and talked in a soft Irish voice. She managed to keep the rooms that were in use in reasonable condition, but if you stepped off the beaten path it was all clutter, and not recently disturbed clutter, either. It was understandable, since she had no help.

The Captain also had plenty to do. He was a sort of chauffeur, sort of butler, sort of gardener, sort of handyman. Immediately after bringing them from Manpool he had been outside driving an antiquated motor mower up and down the lawn which fronted the house and later she had seen him chopping sticks outside the kitchen door. He addressed Mrs Castle with a breezy familiarity that seemed to have a touch of contempt in it, while she for her part seemed anxious to placate him. To Aunt Marion he was deferential in a soldierly way, calling her "Ma'am".

Aunt Marion herself was different from the person they had known on those yearly visits. Not physically: she was the same thin figure with the white wrinkled face and hair coiled above the ears, and she wore a dark brown silk dress Katharine had seen before. Her voice was the same, too – low and reedy, occasionally dropping into an incomprehensible mumble. The difference was in her manner; she was more sure of herself, less awkward. Boring still, perhaps, but not *just* a bore. Katharine realized – she felt she could be – that as a person she was stronger, more definite; she felt she could be formidable, even scaring.

The water was growing cool. Mrs Castle had run the bath, drawing the water from a gas geyser that loomed over the bath like a metal Martian, with levers and knobs for limbs. It had groaned and wheezed horribly during the process and still made small gurgling and whining noises; even if she had known how to operate it she would have been scared to. But the water had not been really hot at the start and was now tepid. Katharine soaped herself quickly and had a go with a long yellow rough-textured thing that she had found in the soap-tray. She decided it was too rough and resorted to her own sponge instead. Then she clambered out and padded across the room to get her towel from the rail on the opposite wall. That would be a chilly journey in winter. She reminded herself that they would not be here then, and was a little surprised to find a shade of disappointment in the thought.

The bath was slow to relinquish its water and she had to wait impatiently for some minutes before she could clean it. After that she went to her room. They had been put in the north wing, the part the Captain said had once been a farmhouse, and she had to go along a corridor and down a small weirdly shaped staircase to reach it. There were gas lamps on wall brackets at intervals but they had been turned down low, giving light not much stronger than a candle's. Her room, she remembered, was on the left, the second. She pushed the door open and found Gwen lying on her bed, staring at her reflection in the oval mirror of the wardrobe.

"You've been a hell of a time," she complained.

"I didn't think I had."

The light here, from twin gas lamps over the fireplace, was brighter. Gwen said,

"Ages. Doesn't all this overgrown gloomy furniture give you the twitch? Just look at that chest of drawers!"

"It's well made," Katharine said. "Very solid. Valuable, I should think, some of it."

"To anyone who wants the rotten stuff, maybe. My room's even worse. And my bed's lumpy."

"Bad luck."

"Yours is, too." She bounced up and down on it. "More so, if anything. What do you make of the Captain?"

"In what way?"

33

"Do you think he *is* a Captain? I mean, that he really was an officer? He doesn't talk like one."

"No," Katharine said. His accent certainly was odd and his grammar uncertain. "In any case, I thought only naval captains used their title. Isn't it majors and above as far as the army is concerned?"

It was a subject on which they had some information. Uncle Geoff, their father's brother, had been an officer in the Royal Engineers for years and in fact had only left the army the previous summer.

"*And*," Gwen said, "he talked about going all the way from Alamein to Algiers with Monty. But the Eighth Army didn't. I remember seeing it in a film on TV. They only went as far as Tunis. Algiers was the Americans. He does look a bit military, though. Stands very straight."

"The Salvation Army, maybe. Perhaps he carried the banner from Alamein to Algiers."

Gwen giggled and Katharine joined in. Gwen said,

"And got cashiered for taking pennies off the drum when he should have been putting them on? Do you think he's sinister?"

"He doesn't look sinister."

"Perhaps he has a hold of some kind on Aunt Marion."

"He doesn't behave towards her as though he had."

"Blackmail. They're always smooth and oily to their victims."

"I wouldn't call him smooth and oily, either. And can you imagine Aunt Marion doing anything someone could blackmail her over?"

"I don't know. Dope-smuggling? After all, this is an isolated house and not many miles from a seaport. She runs an opium ring, maybe. Chinese junks come sailing up the Man and Aunt Marion lurks in the shadows of the

34

Manpool docks and catches the bundles they toss over-
board to her."

They giggled again. Gwen was fun in this mood.
Katharine said,

"I must say, if he is a blackmailer he does things the
hard way. You'd think he'd just call in once a month to
pick up the cash and then fly back to Monte Carlo and
gamble it away in the casino. Bit of a waste to spend this
amount of time chopping and mowing and bringing back
the groceries."

"He *used* to do that; live in Monte Carlo. But on one
visit he fell passionately in love with Mrs Castle, and now
he can't tear himself away from her."

They laughed heartlessly at the notion of someone being
passionately in love with Mrs Castle. Katharine asked,

"Do you think there's a Mr Castle?"

"I suppose there must have been once."

"And he shipped aboard one of those Chinese junks,
maddened by the smell of chop suey and sweet-and-sour
pork after years of near-starvation."

"Cor blimey, yes!" Gwen said. "We certainly didn't
get much for tea. Have you ever heard before of anyone
counting out the slices of bread and butter?"

"Not butter. Margarine."

"Was that it? I thought it tasted funny. If those are the
sort of rations we're going to be on poor old Sarah's
going to feel the pinch. She'll have a waistline like . . . I
mean, she'll have a *waistline* after a month of this."

Katharine, conscience pricked, said,

"I'd better go and see how she is."

"Fast asleep by now, dreaming of chasing chocolate
éclairs. Or being chased by them – what a nightmare!
She'll be all right."

"I think I'll go and look, all the same." She rummaged

in her bag and found a bar of chocolate, which she had managed to save from the stock provided for the journey. "Fourth on the right, isn't she?"

"Yes. Not that it matters. You can't barge in on anyone. There's only us in this part. Ah well. I think I'll go along to my own bed. It *is* a bit better than this. Well, not quite as bad." She yawned. "I feel dead beat. Must be the healthy country air." She made a face. "Another exciting day tomorrow, I suppose."

When she pushed open the door Katharine thought she must have made a mistake: it was dark inside. She could not believe that Sarah would have turned the light off before settling to sleep on her first night in a strange house – particularly a house as strange as this. Then, while she was standing there undecided, she heard a sound, a muffled sob. She called,

"Sarah?"

"Kate? Is it you? I thought . . ."

"Thought what, you halfwit? Why have you put the light out?"

"I didn't. I mean, I was just putting it down a bit, pulling that chain thing the way Mrs Castle said, and it went right out."

"Why didn't you light it again?"

"I couldn't."

"Matches in the table drawer." She felt for them, took a match and struck it against the side of the box. It flared into flame. "I remember Mrs Castle telling you. Or you could have come along to me, or Gwen."

"I . . ." She sat up in bed as Katharine pulled the ring at the end of the chain attached to the seesaw-like bar above the lamp, and the mantle ignited with a pop. Her face was tear-streaked and she was shivering.

36

"Kate," she said, "do you think it is haunted?"

"What, this house? Don't be silly. You didn't pay any attention to the Captain, surely. He was just trying to be funny."

"I could hear noises. Something creaking overhead." She stared up at the ceiling, still fearful. There was a crack even bigger than the one in the bathroom, leading to what looked almost like a hole in the corner. "I thought something might come through."

"A ghost?"

"A mouse. Or a spider."

"Creaking spiders," Katharine said. "What next? Old houses always creak, especially at night. The wood contracts or expands or whatever it is. It's because of differences in temperature. And you ought to know that ghosts don't creak. They either glide silently about or wave their arms and make moaning noises." She sat on the side of the bed. "I don't suppose by any chance you're feeling hungry?"

"I am. Horribly."

She produced the bar of chocolate. Sarah brightened at once, even managing a smile. Unwrapping it, she offered half to Katharine who shook her head. She said,

"The light makes a funny noise, too."

It did, a sort of tiny rattling roar, like metal mice cheering at a distant football match, Katharine thought. She said,

"That doesn't upset you, does it?"

"No. I quite like it. And the light itself, the colour of it – that soft yellow, and the shadows it throws."

"Mrs Castle was telling me it cost Aunt Marion's father a fortune to put gas in. It was when they first had it in Manpool, and they ran a pipe underground for twelve miles just for this house. Apparently he went in for everything modern he could find and didn't mind what it cost him."

"Modern!"

"You've not seen the bathroom yet. Modelled on the one that won the first prize in the Ideal Homes Exhibition of 1888."

"Really? Did they have Ideal Homes Exhibitions as long ago as that?" She saw Katharine smiling and smiled herself. The chocolate was disappearing fast. "I didn't really believe what the Captain said."

Katharine said, "It won't be so bad once we get used to the place."

"No. I suppose not. Only I wish . . ."

"What?"

"It wasn't just the noises. I was thinking about Garance. I almost thought I could hear her crying."

"Not even Garance's yowls could carry for two hundred and fifty miles. I promise you she's all right. Lording it over all the other cats in the Home. Well, ladying it."

"Do you think so?"

"Know so. Are you going to be all right now?"

"Yes, but . . ."

"But what?"

"Would you come in with me for a bit?"

"Sal, really! Just for a while, then. Make room."

She climbed in beside her sister. This mattress was lumpy, too. Sarah snuggled up against her back. She said,

"Do you think Garance will be able to sleep in that little cubbyhole place?"

"I'm sure. Now go to sleep yourself."

It was not long before she did. There was a small convulsive leg kick followed by steady slumbrous breathing. Katharine lay awake, tired but not sleepy. She heard a creak like the ones Sarah had mentioned: it was surprisingly loud and disconnected from the night's silence and she could understand Sarah finding it frightening. So much so that she had not even dared to come in search of her or Gwen but had lain there trembling in the dark. She blamed herself – she ought to have come along to see that Sarah was all right, instead of lingering over her bath and after that sitting gossiping with Gwen.

A creak again, from a different part of the ceiling. She reached up carefully and pulled the gas ring so that the light dimmed. She too liked the colour of the light, its softness and the noise from the burner. And the creaks, once you got over the initial shock, had a comforting quality as well. It was the sound of a house that was settling itself to rest at night, as it had done for hundreds of years before.

The strange feeling of recognition came back, but this surely could have nothing to do with a snapshot carelessly looked at on some forgotten afternoon. Not just recognition, but a sense of being at home. Perhaps she had lived here before, in some previous incarnation. Perhaps she had lain in this bed and heard the troops of the Young Pretender trotting triumphantly southwards – Manpool was one of the cities that had welcomed him with open arms – or disconsolately north on the retreat to Scotland. Or earlier still, with a gale raging outside, and thoughts in one's head of the ships from the Armada being blown and tossed around the coasts of England, some great galleon perhaps foundering at that moment among the rocks and sandbanks that lay outside the Man estuary.

That was silly, of course. Reincarnation was nonsense. But the feeling of comfort was real. She yawned, pressed her face into the pillow's softness and, with a strand of Sarah's hair tickling her nose, fell asleep.

3

Katharine awoke early, to the realization that she was cold; the reason being that Sarah had managed to hog all the bedclothes, leaving her exposed to the dawn air. She had no idea what time it was and decided to go back to her own room and find out. She slipped out of bed, opened the door quietly, and padded down the corridor.

In her room she found her watch and discovered it was just after five o'clock. Much too early to get up; the sensible thing would be to crawl into her own bed and get some more sleep. But she had stopped feeling tired. She went to her window and looked out. The ground was dark and shadowy but she could just make out something that moved – hopped, stood, and hopped again. A rabbit. She found her clothes and dressed quickly. Then, going quietly so as not to disturb anyone, she went downstairs.

She tried the kitchen door first. There were two sets of bolts which groaned loudly as she drew them from their sockets. There was, in addition, a heavy padlock and, she discovered, no key or trace of one. Mrs Castle would probably have a special place for keys; Katharine looked for it but without success. She did find the larder and a wave of emptiness urged her to invade it. Resolutely she closed the door on temptation.

She made next for the conservatory but though this had

a large door at the rear it too was locked. She stood and looked about her. Like the rest of the house it was in bad repair. Panes were missing in several places. There was no sign of the oranges and bananas which Aunt Marion's father was supposed to have planted; everything looked desolate. There were stains where winter's rain and snow had blown in and long low iron contraptions – heaters at one time, she guessed, and probably of the most advanced design – were rusted and clearly useless. On a central shelf stood rows of cactus plants in pots, but the big wooden tubs on the floor, hooped with iron and up to six feet across at the top, were empty. There was nothing else but a jumble of wicker chairs and assorted rubbish. She looked and saw a door at the end which must lead to the tower. It was closed; but opened easily when she tried it.

The room in which she then found herself was in the shape of a circle, about twenty feet in diameter. Windows were small and high above the ground, giving no view out except of grey slits of sky. The walls were covered with a heavy green satiny paper but it was stained by damp and in places peeling away in strips. Some chairs, a long oval table and other items of furniture had been stacked in one corner, ready for a removal which had never taken place. Other than that the room was bare. The floor was parquet but some of the blocks had sprung up.

What principally took the eye was the staircase in the very centre of the room. The stairs were a tight spiral, with a solid handrail in dark oak carved on the outside with galleons. The whole thing ascended to the ceiling and through it. Katharine went to the foot of the stairs and looked up. Even in clear daylight one would not have seen much; there were only shadows and darkness. She put a foot on the bottom stair which creaked heavily and seemed to give under her weight. Climbing, she noticed that worm had got into the wood; the top of the balustrade was eaten away in places.

She climbed the creaking stairs into the darkness, surprised not to feel any apprehension. The sense of being at home came back. Her eyes adjusted to the gloom and then there was light from above. She emerged into a room of the same shape and area as the one below and equally bare. The staircase continued upwards and after a brief inspection she decided to go higher. There would obviously be nothing there but she felt she might as well continue. There might be a view of some sort.

The staircase ended on the next floor and she stepped out through a gap in the handrail. What she saw came as a pleasant surprise. This room was properly furnished, with Oriental-looking carpets on the floor, tables and chairs properly disposed, and book-cases built into the curve of the walls on either side of an enormous antiquated gas fire. The windows were fewer but bigger, looking out in three directions. There were four armchairs, very wide and low and covered in green leather. The book-cases were half empty; on a quick glance the books in them were mostly about sailing ships and naval history. There were pictures on the walls, which were covered in a heavy dull gold paper. For the most part they were very small: ovals and squares and circles showing people, some head-and-shoulders others full-figure, in historical dress. Some of it Elizabethan, she guessed, by the ruffs and doublets. They were all tiny and painted with delicacy and precision. There was a name for paintings like that, she remembered. Miniatures.

Two larger pictures were more in keeping with the carved galleons and the books. Both were seascapes, one showing a sailing vessel scudding on a rough sea with its white sails sharp against a black horizon, the other a similar ship but with sails furled, becalmed in a red sunset. Katharine liked these better and stood for some moments, studying them as well as she could in the half-light. The storm scene was more exciting but she preferred the sunset.

She explored the rest of the room, noting that dust lay thick everywhere. No one could have come here for months, perhaps years. A squat table had its top marked as a chessboard, in white and black squares delicately interlined with red. There was a drawer in the side and she found the chessmen there, white in one compartment, black in the other – huge, intricately carved pieces. A sideboard had painted front panels of men and women who looked French; or at any rate were dressed as she imagined French courtiers dressed before the Revolution. On top a wooden frame held two square cut-glass decanters, both empty though one showing a thick red crust at the bottom. She lifted the stopper and sniffed the rich scent of port wine. The drawers had a jumble of silver knives and forks and spoons and in one of the cupboards were larger objects: teapots, jugs, trays and things. All were badly tarnished, from years of neglect.

On the far side there was a china cabinet, lacquered black and gold, with a red and green dinner service inside and more silver: half a dozen christening cups. Next to it was an oblong trunk in scored and battered wood – oak, she thought, though lighter in shade than the wood of the staircase. And older; she noticed that the corners were pinned with wooden pegs set flush into their surround. The chest had a hasp and padlock, but the padlock was open. The lid came up without difficulty. Inside were old papers, some rolled and tied with ribbon, some loose, and a number of old notebooks with rough brownish leather bindings. She opened one and found the yellowing pages were carefully numbered and interlineated with coarse mauve sheets that appeared to be blotting paper. It was a sort of journal-plus-account book. She read one of the entries:

Mem –
  Sep[r] 7th, 1767, p[d]. M[r]. Heming Collector of the Window tax two Pounds & six Pence due Lady Day, 1766, for one year, according to his Book of Assessm[t] commencing Lady Day 1765.

Turning a few pages she found

Nov[r] 3[d], 1767
  Went wth Mr Pryor to Cuddesden and dined wth the Bishop —.

She had taken the book to the window to get the best of the light. She found on page 35 "A Receipt for the Gout" and next to that "1770: a medicine prescribed for the present distemper am[g]. Horses." And near the beginning a poem, simply titled "A Song":

> A fair delusive face no more
> The prudent Lover shall adore,
>   But shew a nobler Taste;
> Within the Entertainment lies,
> And far remote from vulgar Eyes
>   Virtue & Sense the Feast.
>
> Such a Feast can Patty give,
> Such I willingly receive,
>   For Beauty is but vain:
> The scarlet Roses shall decay,
> The snow-white Lillies fade away,
>   Your Virtue shall remain.

Believe, tho' hoary age should place
Ten thousand wrinkles in thy Face,
   Thy sense would charm the Ear:
May Fortune never shew her Spite
And stop my Ears to mend my Sight,
   Thou'lt lovely still appear.

Composed by the diarist, she wondered? More likely copied from somewhere else because it appealed to him. It was very pretty, and showed an intellectual kind of devotion to want to listen to his lady rather than look at her; but she wondered what Patty's feelings, two hundred years ago, had been if he ever read it to her. Perhaps not quite so enthusiastic.

The light had grown stronger. She put the journal back in the chest, and looked out of the window. The view was over the wooded land where the tree tops tossed in a stiff breeze, to the distant ugliness that was the suburbs of Manpool. The city itself could only be made out as a dim blur, far off. But on a clear day one would see it, and perhaps see the silver ribbon of the Man and the flickering blue of the sea. With a telescope it would probably be possible to pick out ships on the horizon. She thought she knew now why the old man had built this tower. One of the armchairs was still placed near the window; she could imagine him sitting there, staring out, listening in his mind's ear to the roar of surf and the cry of gulls.

They did not see Aunt Marion at breakfast; Mrs Castle took a tray up to her room. The three of them afterwards went exploring, in the first place among the outhouses at the back. Katharine had said nothing about the tower room. She would do so eventually, but she was in no hurry.

There were a lot of buildings which, empty now or piled with assorted junk, had once had their own purposes and functions, some of which could still be discerned. The forge, for instance, cold and bare, with a few iron tongs rusting on hooks set in the walls; presumably at one time the house had had its own blacksmith. It seemed extravagant, but there had probably been a lot of horses. The stables were low and long with what looked like scores of stalls. Some had names carved along the top: Brown Boy, they found, Sergeant and Minstrel.

Sarah said, "I suppose they were the horses that had those places. Look how deeply they're carved – it must have taken ages. Someone must have been very fond of them to do that."

"Cheap labour, more likely," Gwen said. "A whim of the master and some stable boy set to do it at a penny a day, or whatever they paid them in those days. Let's move on. There's nothing here."

Katharine, on her own, would have been content to wander about and let things soak in. What things? She was not sure. It was part of the influence which she was aware of the house exerting on her; as though it were drawing her into itself, easily and peacefully. Not with a siren's lure so much as a friendly acceptance, an acknowledgement of something preordained.

Which was as silly, she told herself briskly, as fantasies about reincarnation. The other two girls showed no signs of feeling like this. Gwen was bored and showed it at the outset, and Sarah became so by degrees. Gwen eventually looked at her watch and said, groaning,

"Not eleven yet. What an all-out swinging holiday this is going to be!"

Katharine said, "Mrs Castle said something about coffee and biscuits at eleven."

46

Sarah looked brighter at the thought.

"Let's go and see. She might do them early. I'm ravenous."

Mrs Castle was in the kitchen but there was no sight or smell of coffee. She said,

"Ah, there youse all are. You'll be wanting something to do, I guess." She smiled at them. "You can be lending me a hand."

She had jobs for everyone. She set Sarah to cleaning knives, Gwen to turning out and tidying the larder, Katharine to putting the kitchen itself to rights. It was a big high-ceilinged room centred round a huge black solid-fuel stove with two ovens. Gwen, with Mrs Castle out of the way for a moment, whispered furiously,

"This gets better and better! No wonder Aunt Marion asked us up here. Free labour's even better than cheap."

The coffee eventually was made but not until half past eleven. It was fresh coffee, not instant, but very weak and they were each offered a single shortbread biscuit to go with it. Katharine slipped hers to Sarah. Mrs Castle went to take Aunt Marion's coffee to her and did not immediately return. Gwen said,

"She'll have more lined up for us when she gets back. I'm getting away while there's a chance."

Sarah went with her. Mrs Castle, when she came back with the tray, said,

"Ah, so they've gone, have they? Well, you're more use than the two of them put together. I've always liked some-one who tackles a job and does it properly. Mrs Mason – she was the first housekeeper I was under – she always made sure a girl was trained to do a job properly. She would never stand for any skimping."

Katharine liked neither the denigration of her sisters – she knew their shortcomings but it was not up to others to point them out – nor the patronizing commendation of herself. This latter was repeated in various forms, between drags on the chain of cigarettes. It went with a galling assumption that Katharine was delighted to be sharing her kitchen tasks. When she was not praising she complained, and this was slightly more preferable. She had been a housekeeper, she said, in really grand houses – not just the gentry but the nobility. She had been used to half a dozen girls working for her, and here she was with no one. There had been a woman that came in but she had given up the previous winter, and had not been replaced.

"Can't you get anyone?" Katharine asked.

"Well, there's all the paraphernalia of the Captain having to let them in at the gate and bring them up to the house, but it's not just that. You can't get people for what Miss Hunston wants to pay. Seventeen and a half pence an hour – there's no one will work for that these days."

"Can't she afford to pay more? I thought . . ."

"It's not a matter of *affording*. Between you and me, she could afford a staff of twenty. It's, well, people have their ways."

Katharine asked, "But why do you stop here, if you don't have proper help?"

"Oh, I couldn't be letting her down, now! I couldn't let someone down who depended on me, the way she does. That's a thing I could never bring myself to do if it meant saving my life."

It was said with great emphasis. Katharine said,

"But it isn't as if my aunt is crippled, or poor or anything. I mean, if you were to leave she would just have to get someone else, and she would realize she would have to pay more for help."

"I wouldn't be dreaming of leaving her." The tone was offended; she went on, in mollifying explanation, "You

48

see, dear, she wouldn't be finding it easy to get anyone who'd put up with things the way I do."

"Is that why the Captain stays?"

Mrs Castle sniffed deeply. "Him?"

"He seems to have a lot of work to do, too."

"Ah, he works when he's in the mood for it." Katharine compared the contemptuous scorn of this with Mrs Castle's ingratiating amiability to his face. "Now then, let's be seeing to the lunch. You can turn the potatoes for me, if you like."

Katharine said, thinking of Sarah who had been known to put away half a dozen large roast potatoes at a sitting and then ransack the fridge for any left over,

"There aren't very many, are there?"

"Miss Hunston can't bear the notion of food being wasted."

It worked out at two small potatoes each. Katharine said,

"I shouldn't think these would be."

Aunt Marion had lunch with them. Rising from the table she said,

"I'll have coffee in my sitting-room. Will you be so kind as to bring it to me, Katharine?"

"Yes, Aunt Marion."

"And bring your own, too. We can have a little chat."

Gwen said, as the door closed behind her,

"Oh, lucky you."

Sarah said, "I suppose there *isn't* any more pudding?"

It had been apple crumble, more crumble than apple and not much of that. Katharine said,

"I know there isn't. Mrs Castle shared it all out."

"I only had about three spoonfuls."

Gwen did not follow her usual custom of deriding Sarah over her appetite, but said,

"That's all I had. Kate, is there any chocolate left?"

"A bar of fruit-and-nut, in my bag in the bedroom. Share it between you."

Sarah said nobly, "We'll save you some."

She shook her head. "No, don't. I'll go and get the coffee for Aunt Marion."

Aunt Marion's personal sitting-room was somehow wedged between the main Georgian section of the house and the older wing. It was really a part of the former, having the same height of ceiling and a well-proportioned window, but in being long and narrow seemed to belong to the latter, with its odd-shaped rooms and corridors and angles that were never quite square.

The walls were lined with furniture – a long china cabinet with dinner and tea services and Dresden figures, two chests of drawers, two sideboards facing each other, several small tables, and a big writing desk of light walnut spliced in with thousands of other fragments of wood in an intricate pattern of marquetry. Aunt Marion sat by the window in a chair that had a semicircular seat, thin jutting-out legs and a high semicircular back. It did not look comfortable but she seemed at ease in it. She said,

"Thank you, Katharine. Put the tray on this table and sit opposite me. I want to look at you."

Katharine did as she was bid, giving Aunt Marion one lump of sugar as requested and a trickle of cream from the small silver jug. She sat down with her own cup, trying not to show the awkwardness she felt. Aunt Marion, appraising her, said,

"You have something of the family resemblance, I think. The mouth and eyes – they remind me of my Aunt Martha a little, though, of course, she was much older then than you are now, and a big woman. Do you think you will like staying here?"

She had been steeling herself as to what she felt she must say, and this was an opening. But her courage failed her. She said merely,

"Yes, Aunt Marion."

"I have not seen as much of you children as I might have wished. There have been reasons for that. Commitments . . ."

She nodded, not paying much attention. She was too concerned with being ashamed of her cowardice. Aunt Marion went on,

"What is the difference in age between you and Gwen? A year?"

"A little over that. Fifteen months."

"Yes. It seems more. Not in the physical sense. She is a nice girl, pretty, with pretty ways and manners, but you have always struck me as a great deal more grown-up. I think you can probably understand adult affairs better. You have been helping Mrs Castle, I believe?"

"A bit. We all were."

"She seems very impressed with you."

The last word was fractionally stressed. Aunt Marion sipped her coffee and Katharine followed suit. There was a silence in which she tried to think of ways of bringing up the topic which was on her mind. It was broken when Aunt Marion said, with an almost fierce abruptness,

"Your Rhodesian cousins – are you acquainted with them at all?"

"No. I scarcely know of them."

"They are nearest to me in family. There are two branches, you understand, and they belong to mine. But this business of a republic . . ."

Katharine had heard her parents talk about the

Rhodesian situation but she was not herself interested in politics and had let it wash unregarded over her head. It was to do with Whites and Blacks – she knew that much – the Whites wanting to keep the Blacks down or something, and her parents were against it. Aunt Marion said,

"It is not a question, of course, of my being in favour of the negroes. My father always said that it would be hundreds of years before they were fit to govern themselves. And I realize that it is not the Queen who decides these things but politicians. My father never trusted politicians. But they, the Rhodesians, have broken the tie. One cannot get over that. They are now foreigners, and by their own act."

This was all excruciatingly boring; and leading them further away from what she wanted to say. She nodded, trying to frame ways of bringing the conversation round. It was not easy.

"My father," Aunt Marion said, "believed in two things above all: family and country. And country, really, came first. In the Civil Wars an ancestor of ours – that would not be your side of the family, of course – disowned and denounced his eldest son for taking up with the Roundheads. I have always thought of everything I inherited from my father as being in trust to his principles. He left more to me than to my brother because I was a girl, unmarried, and Edward was successful in business. Later the business did not prosper so well and some years ago, after his death, his son Robert went farming in Rhodesia. I have always intended to leave everything to Robert."

Katharine said, resigned to an endless monologue, "Yes, Aunt Marion."

"Until this severing of the link with the Crown, that is. I wrote to Robert when it happened, pointing out that if he remained a citizen of what was now not merely a rebellious but a foreign country, I should be obliged to cut him and the children out of my will. I have reminded him of this several times since. He finally wrote back, courteously it is true, refusing to abandon his allegiance to Mr Smith. So I am doing as I promised."

It suddenly and with a shock made sense. Katharine remembered what her father had said that evening in the garden and saw the point towards which they were inexorably moving. She felt her cheeks flushing with embarrassment.

Aunt Marion looked at her, thin lips lifting in a small benevolent smile.

"As I say, you are more mature than your sisters and I can discuss things with you which I could not with them. Your father and you are the nearest family I have, now that Robert has excluded himself and his heirs from it. I have already spoken to my solicitor."

Katharine said, "We don't want . . . I mean . . ."

Aunt Marion ignored her. "I believe in telling people where they stand in financial matters. I cannot bear deception in such things. Arrangements remain to be worked out, but I want you to know that you are to be my heirs. Do you like this house?"

The question found her still floundering. She said, "Yes. I . . ."

"I thought so. One has a feeling. I would not like to think of it being sold, or pulled down. It meant a lot to my father. And has to me."

She was silent, brooding. Katharine gathered her determination. She said,

"Aunt Marion . . ."

"Yes, child?"

"There is something I would like to say."

"Go on."

53

She took a deep breath. "It's about the food . . . the portions are very small." Aunt Marion stared at her in silence. "Last night, and at breakfast, and again at lunch." She hesitated. "I realize it's costing a lot, having us here. We've got some holiday money, and Daddy could send more. I mean . . ."

She stopped, aware how awful it was sounding. Aunt Marion asked,

"Are you hungry, Katharine?"

"I have been a bit. But it's worse for the others, especially Sarah. She's mad on puddings, and there was very little today."

"I have noticed that Sarah is overweight, which is not healthy."

She found herself hating the conversation, and her own part in it, even more than she had anticipated. But she persisted doggedly:

"That may be true, but she is on holiday. And if she were being cut down on puddings, she ought to be getting more protein to make up for it. Oughtn't she?"

"You're a strange girl."

There was no useful response, she felt, that could be made to that, so she kept quiet. The pause lengthened. She began to wonder if she had offended her aunt so much that she might be sent home: her parents would be there till the week-end. Finally Aunt Marion said:

"I will have a word with Mrs Castle. You may go now, Katharine. Take my tray, please."

Katharine went along the corridor with the tray and crossed the hall in the direction of the kitchen. The long-case clock at the foot of the stairs ticked with a slow dragging solemnity. It consoled her with its suggestion of time going on and on, things and occasions being inevitably, in the end, lost and forgotten. She would not always remember that scene with Aunt Marion, nor how badly and baldly her words had sounded.

Suddenly she thought she saw someone, a woman, in the corner of her vision, coming down the stairs which ascended, mahogany-banistered, on the left of the clock. Mrs Castle, she guessed, and turned to ask her where she should put the tray. But there was no one there, nothing but the formless shadows of the staircase. I'm as bad as Sarah, she thought: worse – seeing ghosts where she only imagined them from hearing noises in the night.

Yet although she was still scolding herself, the embarrassment and depression she had been feeling somehow lifted. Inexplicably she felt happy.

4

The weather was blustery and grey, with rain threatening
but not actually putting in an appearance. It came, in full
measure, during the night. They awoke to the sound of it
lashing against their windows, and no promise of relief in
the heavy sky. The distant woods shivered violently,
looking cold and feverish under the lash of wind and
rain.

Gwen and Sarah were desperate for something to break
a housebound monotony that looked as though it must
last all day. Gwen, especially. She seemed on the point of
moving from the dramatic phase of melancholy to the
bitter silent one that was much worse. It was to forestall
this that Katharine introduced them to the tower-room.
She felt a reluctance about doing it, as though she were
yielding up a treasured secret possession. Which was
absurd, she told herself: it was just a room, and in
someone else's house.

They were, at any rate, delighted. Katharine had
brought matches from her bedroom and they found that
the huge old gas-fire still worked. All the long cylinders
of firebrick were broken, some in several places, but the
blue flames from the jets turned them into jagged pillars
of incandescence; and the room into a circle of snugness
that defied the blustering wetness outside. They played

chess (Katharine and Gwen until Gwen tired of losing), and read (Sarah would read anything, even books about naval warfare), and gossiped happily.

Sarah said in the afternoon, as rain gusted more heavily against the windows,

"We didn't have anywhere like this when it rained in Devon."

Gwen offered grudgingly, "It's not too bad really."

"And the food's got better," Sarah said.

"There's more of it," Gwen said. "It's a bit stodgy. Suet pudding . . ."

"You had a second helping," Sarah said, "and finished it."

They wrangled but amicably. Katharine had not talked to them about her conversation with Aunt Marion and said nothing of her protest over food. But clearly Mrs Castle had been given fresh instructions. There had been three rashers of bacon and unlimited toast at breakfast and enough at lunch even for Sarah. Aunt Marion had sat and watched the food disappearing with no visible sign of wincing.

They were cocooned in sounds: outside the growl of wind, scratch and patter and slash of rain, in here the small hoarse roar of the gas-fire. She thought about that. Gas cost money. Should they have asked Aunt Marion's permission before lighting it? But of course they had not even said anything about coming up here. Aunt Marion did not seem to mind what they did as long as they did not disturb her, but if you asked about something there was always the risk of being prohibited.

How rich was Aunt Marion, she wondered? Enough, surely, not to have to worry about paying for food and gas and things like that. Money, she would have thought, mattered less the more you had of it. If this were not so, why want to have it at all?

It was not actually raining the following morning but there was a monotonous chase of low cloud across a sky that had no trace of blue, and the wind had a raw damp edge. The grounds did not look particularly inviting but there was a need to be out in the open after being cooped up for so long. They set out after breakfast on a journey of exploration.

The outbuildings ran back from the old wing. There were gardens in the angle that made with the rest of the house – an ornamental garden near to and a kitchen garden, separated by a hedge, farther away, the whole contained by a crumbling red brick wall topped by rounded blue coping stones that had fallen away in several places. The drive along which the car had come continued past the front of the house and round the side. They followed that in the first place. If the part they had previously seen was in bad condition, this was appalling. It was not merely a question of being potholed: grass and weeds had overgrown it and when they came round to the back they found a few quite large saplings in it.

Katharine said, "I can't see even the Captain driving along this."

Gwen said, "It can't have been used for donkey's years. Look at that sycamore!"

"They grow fast, don't they?"

"But it's ten feet high."

The road, such as it was, took an oblique course towards more wooded country. The woods could be reached more directly by cutting across rough ground, covered with rabbit-cropped grass, thorn bushes and at one point a brilliant patch of heather. They headed for that on

Sarah's insistence and stopped while she picked some. Then they went on into the woods. Where the trees began there were thick clumps of bramble, at the moment bright with white flower. They would be laden with berries eventually but, as Sarah remarked wistfully, not until after they were back in London.

Gwen, as they entered the woods, went into one of her wild moods. She darted in different directions, swung with Tarzan yells from low branches, and held progress up while she climbed a tree. She called down nonsense to the others about things she pretended she could see: a herd of elephants thundering down on Hunston House, Aunt Marion riding sidesaddle on a unicorn, Mrs Castle being carried away, kicking and screaming, by a pack of red-bottomed apes . . .

She came down at last and they went on, wandering with no particular intent. The trees were thick in places and at others opened out into small glades with more signs of rabbit occupancy. In one of these they found bushes, low to the ground, hung with small blue fruit. Sarah wanted to try them but Gwen was opposed to it: they might be poisonous. Katharine took one and sampled it.

"I thought so," she said. "Bilberries."

"They're all right, then?" Sarah asked.

"Lovely with cream. I had some once at Mary Temple's house."

"We could take some back for tea."

"Bet we wouldn't get any cream out of old Castle," Gwen said.

"We haven't anything to carry them in, anyway," Katharine pointed out.

So they picked and ate them on the spot, and wandered on with lips and fingers stained with blue. The woods seemed to stretch endlessly. Sarah said,

"How far have we walked? Must be miles and miles."

"Not really," Katharine said. "We've been drifting around but I wouldn't think we've covered more than a couple of miles. We'd better not go too far."

"Why not?" Gwen asked. She looked at her watch. "Loads of time before lunch."

"We might get lost."

"We won't. I've got a sense of direction."

"Yes," Katharine said. "We noticed it the day you got lost in Bideford."

That had happened on their previous holiday. Gwen said,

"That was different. Anyway, we're bound to come to the wall eventually. We can always follow it round."

"The circumference of a circle," Katharine said, "in case you've forgotten, is $2\pi r$. Say the radius is two miles, that makes it about thirteen miles round. I suppose we might get back for tea."

"Oh, don't be such a grinding bore! Besides, I can always climb a tree to find out where we are."

There was an oak near by with accessible lower branches. Gwen ran to it and hauled herself up.

Katharine called to her,

"Never mind. I'm pretty sure I know the way back. It's just that we could get lost if we went on a long way."

Gwen shouted down, "I *can* see the house. The tower, anyway. Hang on, there's something in the other direction as well."

Sarah said, "Another herd of elephants, I suppose." She added, with the grown-up indulgence she sometimes used towards her elder sister, "Gwen does get a bit imbecilic sometimes."

"I can see the wall," Gwen called. "And something else. I'm coming down."

She jumped the last six feet and sprawled on the damp ground. Katharine noticed a brown smear of mud down the leg of her blue trousers. It was typical of her that, normally extremely fussy about her appearance, she should suddenly go climbing trees and falling about. She said sharply,

"We'd better start back."

"No, not yet," Gwen said. "I told you, I could see the wall . . ."

"Thrills," Sarah said. "Who wants to look at a wall?"

"And a building," Gwen said. "A lodge, I suppose, like the one where we came in. There looked as though there were gates there, too."

"A ruin like the other one, I suppose," Katharine said.

"No," Gwen said, "I don't think so."

"Well, you wouldn't be able to see whether it was or not."

"It looked as though there were smoke coming from the chimney. So it can't be a ruin. Anyway, I'm going to investigate."

She set off and Katharine and Sarah followed her. The trees thinned in that direction and after about twenty yards they came on what was obviously a continuation of the road which they had abandoned shortly after leaving the house. It was overgrown by bushes and weeds and a few small trees but its identity was plain enough. There had obviously, Katharine realized, been two gates in use at one time; but one had been abandoned, along with the road leading to it. Then what was all this about smoke coming from the chimney of the lodge? Gwen's imagination? Or squatters from outside?

They followed the road, Gwen leading the way still. Suddenly, on the right, the ground opened up completely past a small tangled hill of brambles. Immediately ahead there was cultivated ground. Katharine saw rows of potatoes, some of them cleared, beans, peas, onions and cabbages. The plots were neat and tidy, and had been weeded. Her father would have approved. So the place must be occupied. But by whom? Would squatters go in for gardening?

Sarah gave an exclamation of pleasure and Katharine, following the direction of her gaze, saw something else. On this side of the garden, beyond a thin screen of trees, there was more open ground, something like a pasture. The grass was quite thick there, and a goat was cropping it.

It lifted its head and stared at them with cold yellow eyes. It was on a tether. Sarah, with her usual reaction to almost any kind of animal, ran towards it and stroked it. It pushed its long narrow head against her in a butting gesture that was presumably intended to be affectionate. Sarah, at any rate, interpreted it as such and put her face down to its neck. It was a nanny, heavy with milk.

Gwen looked towards the cottage. She said,

"I was right. Someone is living there."

It was a twin to the one they had already seen on the far side of the estate: a small square box of red brick topped by a shallow blue slate roof. There were two windows on this side, quite small ones. But they had glass in them instead of being boarded up and the frames were painted primrose yellow. There were bright red curtains, too, and Katharine saw that the door, which was in the wall that abutted on the gates, was light blue with a brass knob that gleamed despite the morning's greyness. Whoever was living there was fond of colour. The gates, on the other hand, were not only closed but had been reinforced at some distant time with barbed wire, which was as heavily rusted as the gates themselves.

Gwen started to go forward, taking a path that led alongside the cultivated land. Katharine said,

"You can't . . ."

"Can't what?"

"We can't just barge in."

"Why not? It's Aunt Marion's land."

"Even so . . ."

"I'm going to have a closer look. You do as you like."

Katharine followed her, reluctant but also curious. There was a wooden bench against the wall between the two windows, oddly painted in green and golden yellow splotches. Gwen went to a window and peered inside. Uneasily Katharine did the same.

The interior was on the spartan side but again colourful. She saw a couple of yellow chairs and a simple kitchen table with a plain scrubbed top but with its legs painted green. A Welsh dresser, striped green and yellow, had tins and packets of food on its shelves as well as a few plates and cups. Floorboards, like the table top, were scrubbed and in places covered with squares of orange and black matting. There was a small sink under a window that faced this one, and an old-fashioned grate with a barred fire and an oven door – but the door was crimson, not black. It was the ceiling, weirdly, that was black. The walls in contrast were a sharp white, what could be seen of them. For the most part they were hung with paintings, a few framed but the majority simply squares of un-mounted canvas.

There was no sign of an occupant, or occupants. Gwen said,

"Must be out. Or in the other room.' She ran to the second window and called, "Not there, either. It's the bedroom."

Katharine said, "We really mustn't . . ."

She stopped in a quick shock of surprise. The path ran along the side of the house and disappeared round a clump of elderberry bushes, very high and laden with fruit. Looking past Gwen, who was bending forward by the window, she saw a figure standing just this side of the bushes, watching them: a man.

He said, "Well, then, young ladies. What can I do for you?"

The first impression had been a bit alarming – patched jeans, a black jersey rolled up under the neck, and a great deal of gingery brown beard – but the voice was reassuring. It was pleasant, well modulated and unmistakably southern and respectable. Gwen, straightening up and looking round hurriedly, said,

"We were wondering if we could beg a glass of water."

Katharine would not herself, she knew, have had the readiness or the presence of mind to come up with an excuse like that. The man stared at her admiringly.

"Are you blushing, or have you been running? Real roses in those cheeks. Of course you could have a glass of water but may I suggest a cup of tea instead? My water's not all that good and tea would improve it."

Gwen said,

"If you're sure we're not bothering you . . ."

"No bother. I'm delighted to have visitors. Surprised *and* delighted. You're the first I've had since I've been here."

"There are three of us."

"So I saw. The third being the one with her arms round Ludmilla. Call her to come in as well, but she'd better leave Ludmilla where she is. She's most affectionate and would willingly join us for tea but one has to draw a line somewhere."

He had a thin face, not really attractive, with eyes set close together and a high narrow forehead. His skin was well tanned, presumably from being out of doors a good deal: there must have been more sun here earlier in the summer than there was now. His smile was nice, Katharine thought: open but perhaps just a little anxious, as though wanting to please you. How old was he? Over thirty. Thirty-five, maybe.

Gwen called to Sarah, and the man led the way round the side of the house. Gwen said to him,

"How long is it?"

"How long is what?"

"That you've been here."

"Over a year. This is my second summer."

"All by yourself?"

"Except for Ludmilla, and the hens. Funny how strange voices sound when you don't hear them much. I talk to myself, but it's different."

"How can you stand it," Gwen asked, "– being on your own?"

She spoke with conviction; she was not someone who could tolerate her own undiluted company for long. He said,

"It's not too bad. Good for my soul, probably."

There was a brimming water-butt beside the door and an enclosed metal tank, painted rose-pink but with redder stains showing through at the edges, fastened on the wall. He tapped it as he passed.

"That's why I don't recommend the water. Collected from the roof, and there's a little rust inside as well as out. You can boil it, of course, and I keep a kettle on the hob. Won't take a minute to brew some tea. No China, I'm afraid, only Indian. And if you want milk it will either be out of a can or out of Ludmilla."

He stood to one side and motioned them in. The door led directly into the living-room. He said,

"Two chairs are an unnecessary luxury under normal circumstances – one of them very nearly went for firewood during the winter when I was laid up with a fever for a few days – but a bit inadequate for guests. Still, the floor's clean and I often sit on it myself. It's not a bad idea to take a mouse-eye view of the world occasionally. Now, I'm Hugo Burton – Hugo, please. Tell me who you are."

They introduced themselves. He said,

"Katharine, Gwen, Sarah – fine, I've got that. And how's Miss Hunston, and all at Hunston House?"

"You know her?" Katharine asked.

"My landlady? One can scarcely say landlady, though, when one pays no rent. Maybe benefactress is better. You will be the London cousins."

Katharine said, half accusingly, "Then you do know her quite well, if you know who we are."

"Not really." His smile was a frank one, especially in contrast with the slightly foxy look his face had otherwise. "Something that was said, I forget by whom."

"Surely it could only have been said by Aunt Marion?"

He had moved the kettle from the side plate to a position directly over the fire and now tipped hot water from it into an old-fashioned teapot, high and square, its cracked white glaze painted with purple and red pansies. After swilling it round he tossed the water out through the open door.

"Excuse my primitive way of life," he said. "No, it need not have been your Aunt Marion. It might have been Mrs Castle, or the Captain. With Mrs Castle the more probable. Her tongue tends to wag, as you may already have noticed."

"So you've *lived* at the House?"

"No. I used to visit occasionally. But the Captain and I found each other, shall we say, a little unsympathetic. So I retired fully to my little cottage, my 'Walden'. I haven't seen any of them for a long time."

Gwen said, "All these paintings. Did you do them?"

"Guilty as charged. You are looking for an easel, paints and such? In that cupboard in the corner. I try to keep the place tidy. That was a gun cupboard, by the way. The gamekeeper's gun cupboard."

"Gamekeeper?"

"I gather this gate was hardly ever used even at the beginning. But the old boy kept his own game – liked to go out and knock off a pheasant for the pot. So he installed the gamekeeper here. His spirit wakes me up when the moon is full, and I lie awake listening for poachers in the bushes."

Sarah said, fascinated, "Does it really?"

Hugo smiled again. "*Un façon de parler.* I'm sure you all do French at school. No, not as a ghost or anything like that, but I think little bits of people hang around in places they've been fond of. Places like this, of course, not semi-detached villas in the suburbs. I suppose more than one gamekeeper lived here, but I roll them up into one. I think of him as Charlie – old Charlie with mutton-chop whiskers and a slightly drooping moustache, smoking thick black twist in an old briar pipe he cut out himself. I can even smell it sometimes on a calm evening."

He made the tea with experienced economical movements.

"Two minutes to draw. I approve of Charlie and I have a feeling he approves of me. Which is strange when you consider how different our ways of life and habits must have been. I think of him as a man fond of his meat – a good hand with a rabbit stew or at grilling one of the pheasants old Hunston didn't get. Whereas I am not a flesh-eater at all. I nourish myself on the fruits of the earth. And the veg, of course. Plus a few dairy products. I must confess to being an egg-eater, too, on a fairly hefty scale."

Gwen asked, "Do you grow everything yourself?"

He poured tea into mugs of different shapes and colours.

"I'd like to say yes, but I must be honest. The road's about a mile away, across the fields." He gestured to the window on his left and Katharine saw that there were no houses in that direction. Outside wheat waved in the wind and in the distance she saw brown earth and a tractor moving slowly across it. Hugo said,

"I climb out of my window and get a hitch into the city when necessary, and exchange a couple of paintings for provisions."

Sarah asked with interest, "At the grocer's?"

"Not directly. The paintings go to a dealer who pays me a pound or two and very likely puts them away, to sell for five or ten thousand when I'm dead and famous. Excuse me while I nip outside for the milk."

While he was gone, Gwen said,

"Isn't he *super*? I mean, an artist – and living like this . . ."

There was a clucking and squawking as he returned and through the door they had a glimpse of a feathery body, just airborne. Hugo carried a blue jug and a can of evaporated milk.

"One of my hens," he said. "I'm fond of them, but not in the house and they're always having to be discouraged. Hetty, in particular. If I didn't take a firm stand she'd be laying eggs in the bed. The jug contains goat milk. I like

68

it, but there are some who find it, well, pungent." He produced a small red knife full of gadgets and punched two holes in the can. "Milk, ladies?"

Gwen said, "I'll have the goat milk."

"A person who believes in trying new things," Hugo said approvingly. "I have something of a weakness that way myself."

Gwen blushed with pleasure. Katharine said, "Have you always lived like this, Mr Burton?"

"Hugo, please. Burton makes one think of slick city suitings, and the poisonous processed beer they make nowadays, and people buying vulgar great diamonds for their wives. Do call me Hugo."

Katharine said, "Well, yes, of course." He cocked his head on one side, smiling and waiting. "Hugo."

"Good! Now I've forgotten the question. I have a shocking memory altogether. Oh yes – have I always lived like this? Indeed, no. I've turned my hand to a few things in my time. I was at sea a couple of years as a wireless operator. That was after spending two years in the army, at the same trade. I had a spell in Australia as a farm labourer, only they call them stockhands which sounds nicer. I've even sheared sheep, though I must admit I wasn't very good at it. And I've been in the Stock Exchange, and I've sold encyclopaedias, and I've been an instructor in a driving school and I've worked for exactly two hours on a broilerhouse chicken farm – that was when I finally made up my mind about flesh eating – and I've done a season as a lifeguard at a holiday resort and eighteen months with a travelling circus: I was put in charge of the elephant which was an important post and, I found, quite a pleasant one. There are probably a few more things I've done but I can't call them to mind at this moment."

Sarah said, "You really had an elephant to look after?"

"Yes. I was very sorry to part company with her. A real lady, Anna. But I got tired of the constant moving about. I felt a need to sit still a while, and think."

"Was that why you came here?" Katharine asked.

"Well, not exactly. The encyclopaedias came immediately before this. I found myself in this part of the country and I called on your aunt. We have a" – he smiled – "well, a long standing but distant connection, you might say. I told her how tired I was of racketing about, that I wanted to find some quiet spot far from the madding world, and paint. Generously she told me I could help myself to this little haven. It was a ruin, of course, and I've done a fair bit of renovating as you can see. Still, I was immensely grateful."

"But you don't visit her?"

"No." He laughed. "And she doesn't call on me. In my case, it might look as though I were trespassing on her kindness and I wouldn't like to do that. She's a woman of firm principles, you know. She doesn't like things to be cluttered up with emotions, likes them clear." Katharine thought of what her aunt had said about the nephew in Rhodesia, and had an inkling of his meaning. "She performed a small disinterested act of charity, I thanked her, and that's that. It's not as though we have a great deal in common, really."

"Nor," Gwen said with feeling, "do we."

"Ah, well, it's different in your case, isn't it? How long are you staying with her?"

"A month. We don't want to."

Katharine said, "Gwen —"

Hugo laughed. "Never mind, I won't tell. And I think that's a healthy reaction. But you'll probably like it more than you imagine. And I hope when you can't think of

70

anything else to do you'll come over here and say a few kind words to Ludmilla and me."

Gwen in her satisfaction took a deep swallow of her goat-milk-flavoured tea. It was marvellous, Katharine thought, to watch the way she controlled her instinctive shudder. She herself said,

"But if you want to be on your own, away from people, we'd be a nuisance."

He gave a small bow. "There are people and people. And after this long isolation I'm glad of a change from my own company. Do please come. As a matter of fact, I'd like to paint you – all three of you together."

Katharine glanced at the nearest picture on the wall. It showed a mass of red and purple writhing shapes against a black background marked here and there with silver star splinters.

"No," Hugo said, "not that sort of thing. More like that." He pointed to another picture. "Though the subjects will be prettier, of course."

The painting was one of the goat, Ludmilla, with a tuft of grass hanging from her jaws, and was lifelike in an only slightly exaggerated way: her ears and her yellow eyes looked a bit too big.

Gwen said, "Will you really?"

"It will be a joy."

Katharine said, "We must be getting back now."

"Not just yet," Gwen said.

Katharine gave her sister a hard stare.

"Yes, we must."

Gwen stared mutinously back. Hugo said easily,

"I won't try to keep you; but I will rely on your coming again. Now, it's a promise, isn't it?"

Gwen said, "Yes, it is, Hugo."

·   ·   ·   ·   ·

Katharine washed her hands in the bathroom before lunch. The water supply to the hand-basin was cold, and she rubbed and scrubbed furiously to make up for that. The soap was hideous red carbolic. She wished she had brought some from home and wondered if it would be too fussy to write for it. Or she might be able to buy a bar if they got into the city with the Captain on one of his shopping expeditions.

She was thinking prosaically of this as she came out into the corridor. The first strange thing was the feeling of silence. Feeling was the right word because there was a sense almost of being touched by it, confined and pressed close inside a circle, a tunnel, something that cut her off completely from the ordinary world. And yet everything looked the same: the worn green carpet, framed silhouette drawings, gas brackets on the wall, mahogany tallboy at the top of the stairs.

All these and something else. She knew it was the figure she had seen before: a woman who was quite old, over fifty certainly. She was in shadow but seemed to be wearing a grey dress, high at the neck. She stood for a moment looking at Katharine and about fifteen feet from her. Then she began to come forward. She was limping heavily as she walked.

Even before she realized that she could actually see the corner of the tallboy through the shadowy figure, Katharine knew that this was – really was – a ghost. What amazed her was her own reaction: she felt curiosity but no fear. The woman seemed to smile and she found herself smiling in response. Then in the distance she heard Gwen's voice calling to Sarah, and the tunnel of silence went and the figure with it.

5

The Captain raised no objection to their going shopping with him; in fact said he would be glad of the company. They left the house about ten o'clock and the old estate car crawled along the dilapidated drive to the gates and there was the familiar business of stopping the car and opening, driving through and locking up again.

The girls had hoped to be taken into the centre of Manpool but were quickly disabused of that idea. The Captain took them to a suburban shopping centre, not much more than a mile away, and parked in a side street. He said,

"We leave again at eleven-thirty sharp, righty-o? Which means I want you three young ladies sitting in the car by eleven-twenty-five." He removed his peaked cap and laid it carefully on the driver's seat, as though stationing a watchdog. "Miss Hunston likes to have half an hour with her newspapers before lunch."

He had explained that he collected *The Times* for her on these trips, two or three issues at a time, and also her mail from the local post office. Gwen said,

"Couldn't we go back by bus?"

"Maybe you could," the Captain said, "if there was one went anywhere near the House. Eleven-twenty-five it is."

Gwen grumbled but in fact the place was dull and its resources severely limited. They wandered about looking in desultory fashion at the small shops and spent ten minutes or so in Woolworth's. Sarah had been hoping to find a public library but had no luck. They asked eventually and were told the nearest branch was at Marston, which was apparently another suburb.

They got back to the car five minutes ahead of the time specified. Goods of various kinds were piled in the back but there was no sign of the Captain. Ten minutes later, on the dot, he emerged from the Saloon Bar of the Stag's Head on the corner of the road, wiping his mouth with the back of his hand.

"Can't even have a drink in peace," he said as he got into the car and put his cap on, adjusting the driving mirror to make sure it sat at the right angle.

Gwen said, "Why not?"

"Chattering away," the Captain said. "Like a lot of bloody blackbirds. Excuse me, but it makes you sick. Chattering and giggling and laughing. In the Saloon Bar, too. One of them had a mouth-organ. He made as though he was going to play it a couple of times. I'd have made sure he got kicked out if he did. Big Joe in the old days would have had them out anyway, but the chap who runs the place now doesn't seem to mind what sort he gets in there."

He hooted lengthily at a small car dithering in front of them on a roundabout. As it got out of the way, he went on,

"You always used to get them round the docks, of course, but now they're all over the place – spreading out everywhere. It was the West Indians first, and then the Pakkis. West Indians, this lot were – they make more noise than the others. The Pakkis are quieter. They creep

74

about, hoping you won't notice how many of them there are, or what they're up to."

Gwen said furiously, "You despise people because their skins are a different colour! They're just as good as we are."

"Better, sometimes," the Captain said. "One of the finest men I've ever known was a Ghurka soldier. Not much more than five feet tall and brave as ten lions. And you know what Kipling says, in 'Gunga Din':

> For all 'is dirty 'ide,
> 'E was white, clear white inside ..."

"And is he supposed to take that," Gwen asked with angry sarcasm, "as a compliment?"

The Captain unperturbed went on quoting:

> "Though I've belted you an' flayed you,
> By the livin' Gawd that made you,
> You're a better man than I am, Gunga Din!"

"Of *course*," Gwen said. "As long as he doesn't object to being belted and flayed now and then."

"You don't understand these things," the Captain said cheerfully. "You will, when you've had the experience. You've not had it like a chap I know did – living in a quiet little street in a nice house he'd bought over twenty years on mortgage. And then suddenly they're all round him, sleeping six to a room, frying food and singing and yelling blue murder at three in the morning."

Gwen said, "All right, that was bad luck. They've got to get used to living in England, to our ways of life. It's bound to take time."

"Time? Four or five hundred years, maybe. And we'll all be off our rockers by then. Ever hear that story about the Zulu who asked the Lord why he made him so black?

'To protect your skin from the tropical heat, my son,' the Lord said. 'And why did you make me tall?' 'So you could look out over the high jungle grass.' 'And why did you give me a strong right arm?' 'So you could throw your spear and slay the wily antelope for your meat. Have you any other questions, my son?' 'Only one, Lord,' the Zulu said. 'For Gawd's sake, what am I doing here in Manpool?'"

The Captain went off into prolonged hoots of laughter at his own joke, to which Gwen responded with bitter silence. He did not seem to mind but changed the subject. He talked about Manpool, the way it had spread out between the wars. He had known it in the twenties, he said, and all this part had been countryside, with scarcely a house in sight. Good farming land. Dairy, for the most part, with green fields and herds of cows – Guernseys and Jerseys and Friesians. And one farmer had bred a special kind of goat, called the Manpool Marvel. It had all gone.

Sarah asked, "Do you think Ludmilla might be a Manpool Marvel?"

"Ludmilla?"

"The goat Hugo keeps."

"Oh, him." The tone was scornful. "Has he been hanging round the House again?"

Katharine said no, they had found the other lodge by accident. Gwen said, indignation flaring to a new peak,

"What's wrong with Hugo? *I* like him."

"I'm not surprised," the Captain said. "He's smooth enough. Those tricky ones generally are."

"What's tricky about him?" Gwen demanded. "He lives by himself, not bothering anyone. And he paints really great pictures."

"I wouldn't know about pictures. Lives by himself?

76

Well, I suppose he has done since I gave him a flea in his ear for hanging round the House. Always on the scrounge. Mrs Castle got properly fed up with him."

"Did Aunt Marion know," Katharine asked, "about your giving him a flea in the ear?"

"Know? Of course she knew!"

"But she let him stay on at the lodge? I mean, it is her property."

The Captain paused before answering. He said,

"When Miss Hunston says something she doesn't go back on it. She told him he could live there as long as he wanted, and so he can. Her word's as good as her bond. She's a very straight woman, your aunt."

Gwen said, "Anyway, he's put it back into decent condition from being a ruin."

"Has he? I wouldn't know. I've not been visiting."

"And he keeps it marvellously clean and tidy."

"I suppose he might be some good as a housemaid. Not as much else."

"It's like people with black skins," Gwen said. She had raised her voice angrily. "Just because you don't like artists . . ."

"Nothing to do with art," the Captain said. "It's him I don't like. And the reason is that I don't trust him. And the reason for that is that I've had enough experience of life to know the kind of man you can trust and the kind you can't."

"As an officer in the army, I suppose," Gwen said.

The remark was sharply pointed with sarcasm but he appeared not to notice. He nodded cheerfully.

"That's as good a place as any for learning to sort out the wheat from the chaff."

"In the Western Desert," Gwen added, pulling a derisive face behind him.

"Those were the days," the Captain said. "Hard living, hard fighting. Men depending on each other because they had to."

"Those are the goodies, are they?" Gwen asked. "The hard living, hard fighting ones? Dependable – because they have to be."

"Everything was clean," the Captain said. "We knew what comradeship meant. And the Hun was a clean fighter, same as us."

Gwen said firmly, "I like Hugo."

"I suppose he's got pretty manners," the Captain said, "with young ladies."

Gwen bit back whatever she had been about to say and stared out of the window. Katharine asked,

"When was it that you had this, well, argument with him?"

"Argument? There was no argument. I just told him I didn't want to see him up at the House again. I didn't go into what might happen if I did. I think he cottoned on, all right – he's no fool. When? Beginning of summer. Couple of months back."

Hugo had said he hadn't seen any of them for a long time, and she had taken that to mean something like a year, six months anyway. But two months could seem long enough to someone living by himself.

They came through the council houses to wasteland and the sight of the wall and the gates. The car slowed to a crawl.

"Here we are again," the Captain said.

Aunt Marion said, "Do your parents permit you to have wine?"

Katharine said, "We have some at Christmas, and on Mother's birthday."

"Pour yourself a small glass of sherry."

Katharine did so. Aunt Marion was sipping the gin and tonic water which, according to Mrs Castle, she had every evening before dinner, and which today Katharine had been required to bring to her in her sitting-room. Aunt Marion said,

"My father allowed me a small glass of sherry daily from my fourteenth birthday."

There was a silence which Katharine did not attempt to break. The girls had had their high tea. Aunt Marion dined alone in the evening, in the big dining-room with seven empty chairs at the long walnut table and her tiny distorted reflection looking at her from the convex mirror with the golden eagle drooping a golden ball over it.

Aunt Marion said, "I do not care for the dress Gwen was wearing today. Not merely because it is too short. The material is plainly shoddy. It will look like a rag in no time. Your own is much more sensible."

Katharine still did not say anything. Gwen had a knack, which she had long envied, of occasionally talking her mother into letting her have slightly exotic garments. They looked well on her, too. On the few occasions that Katharine had managed a similar success the dress had looked revolting when she got it home and tried it on.

"You are not at all like her," Aunt Marion said, "in character or temperament." There was a note of approval in her voice which Katharine felt she could have done without. "But of course that is not uncommon in families. All my brothers were quite different."

Katharine asked, surprised, "You had more than one?"

"Five," Aunt Marion said. "But two died as babies, and Paul was killed in a hunting accident when he was thirteen, and Andrew in the war. Their pictures are on the wall there."

Katharine went to look at them. They were in matching silver frames but the photographs were of different sizes. Two were small ovals of round childish faces. The third showed a boy in riding clothes, holding a hunting crop across his knee; he was dark and thin-faced, smiling confidently at the camera. The fourth was a young man in army officer's dress, large and fair, looking bewildered and a bit sad.

They must all, she realized, have lived here, in this house. She wondered just what Aunt Marion remembered of them, of those far-off times – whether it was still sad to think of them, and of them dying so young. A fifth frame had a photograph, in colour, of a fleshy middle-aged man. That would be the one that survived, father of the disinherited Rhodesian. He seemed less real than the others, in their fading black-and-white and sepia.

Aunt Marion began to talk about them: descriptions, small anecdotes, a rambling account of the way things had been here when she was a girl. By the time she was her own present age, Katharine realized, all but that one had died. Much of her talk was incomprehensible, full of unexplained references, wandering round and away from the original point. She did not find it boring, though. Something came through which fascinated her: a sense of what life had been like then – enclosed, well ordered, seemingly secure. And the house itself was part of the story. It was here that these things had happened: the house had watched and listened to them and wrapped them somehow inside itself.

"We were brought up kindly," Aunt Marion said, "but strictly also. Our pocket money was a penny a week. A penny was worth more, of course, but it was still very little. And I remember that once I was allowed to have a pet rabbit. I had begged for months and I was given it on my birthday. A white one, with long fur and big ears. Some time later I forgot to feed it one morning. It was fed by Mrs Johnson, the housekeeper, and my father found out. He told me that if I forgot again I would lose it. I remembered for weeks, months perhaps, and then something happened and I was excited and forgot again. So he gave my rabbit to Mrs Johnson."

"Did she want it? I mean people don't usually want pet rabbits when they are grown up."

"I believed she did, which was all that mattered. I went weeping to her and begged for it back, and she went to my father and asked him if she could give it to me. He said yes, providing I paid her for it. He put its price at sixpence, which meant that for the next six weeks I had to give my pocket money to Mrs Johnson as soon as I received it from him."

"And she took it?"

"She had no choice. It would have cost her her place to refuse."

Katharine said, "It seems rotten to me. And unfair."

Aunt Marion shook her head. "No, not unfair. I had been warned."

"Even so —. But I was thinking of the housekeeper. Unfair to her, making her take pennies from you and threatening to sack her if she didn't."

"You don't understand, child. No threats were made. My father was the master, and the master's word was law in everything, however small. One learnt discipline. And one learnt the value of money."

Katharine asked, "Does money have value? I mean, I know you can buy things with it, but does it matter as much as all that?"

"It gives order to life," Aunt Marion said. "And it provides a test of people. People often claim to be indifferent to money, but are not so when it comes to the point."

Katharine thought of her father's words in the garden. She felt herself flushing and looked away. She said,

"It was through money that your father could make the housekeeper take the pennies from you, even though she probably hated doing it. If that's a way of testing it seems to me a bad one."

She thought her aunt would resent the criticism of her father and perhaps be angry with her. There had been a sort of intention of provoking that in her mind, as an act of definace against the inheritance that had been talked about last time. But Aunt Marion did not react. She said, in a thin distant voice,

"A test, and a hard one. One learns, as a child, to live meagrely, to accept hardships. Not the hardships of the poor, but real enough. I cried all night when the rabbit was taken from me, and losing six weekly pennies was a reprieve – something to be glad for. Then, having learned to master oneself, one finds oneself with a mastery over money. A great deal in my case, because only Edward and I were left. I was thirty when he also died. There had been men who said they wanted to marry me, but I preferred to stay with my father. There were men after his death as well, and I was alone then, of course. I became engaged twice, but each time I broke it off. The first time after I heard my fiancé telling someone, another man, about his business: that it needed an infusion of capital to be prosperous. I knew where the infusion must come from and realized what my true significance was to him. With the second there was no such critical moment; just a growing awareness that my money was more important to him than I was."

She paused. Katharine said,

"How horrible."

"Not horrible. It is the way people are. One ought not to expect too much."

"Horrible for you, I meant."

"Not that, either." She smiled faintly. "It forced me to realize that I did not need them as much as I had thought – something that it was surely better to understand before marrying rather than later. I have no regrets."

But you should have, Katharine wanted to say: the money tyrannized over you as much as over those two men – if it meant more to them than the human person so it did to you. She could not say it. Not because of the reaction it might provoke but because it was too plainly true and, if understood, too wounding.

Aunt Marion straightened up, as though gathering herself for the return from reverie to reality. She looked at the small watch on her wrist, gold and edged with green and white stones that gleamed in the early evening dimness.

"Almost time for dinner. Take the tray through for me, Katharine, will you? Are you always called Katharine? The name is not shortened?"

Katharine said, "Yes. People call me Kate."

"Not Kitty?" Katharine shook her head. "I had a friend at school whose name was Kitty. I went away to school, you know. My father was more modern in his views than you may think. I quite liked it but I was always glad to be home. If you don't mind, I will call you Kitty."

She did mind, but she had a sudden picture of Aunt Marion as a girl, coming back at term's end to the place she loved; and an unexpected feeling of closeness to her. She said,

"If you like, Aunt Marion."

.　　.　　.　　.　　.

Sarah said, "Can't we have Ludmilla in the picture?"

"No," Hugo said, "for two reasons. The first is that I plan to do a study of three charming young ladies, and a nanny-goat doesn't strike me as an entirely suitable prop. In fact, it would throw the whole effect out. And then, I am going to sit you here, indoors. That way we'll be free of interference from the weather. It's not raining today but I shall need more than one sitting, a lot more. I can toss my fantasy-abstracts off fairly fast, but I have to take my time on portraits. And I have even stronger objections to that goat in the house than to hens."

He arranged them round the table, Katharine and Gwen on chairs and Sarah kneeling on a cushion on a wooden box he had brought in. They were to be staring inwards at a crystal ball, represented by the spherical shade of an oil lamp which was his means of lighting his dwelling. A corny idea, Katharine thought privately. Gwen, who normally would have had the same reaction but expressed it a lot more pungently, said how marvellous it was. Hugo, obviously, could do no wrong. Katharine noticed that from the angle at which he was sketching them, drawing in soft pencil on cartridge paper pinned to a board, she and Sarah would be profile or part-profile, Gwen full face. Well, that was fair enough. She *was* prettier.

She felt a bit guilty towards Hugo. She and Gwen had argued about the Captain and his criticisms. Gwen said it was obvious the Captain resented Hugo for being artistic and more intelligent than he was. Katharine, to start with, was merely annoyed with Gwen for getting so worked up about it all; it was typical of her to go to such an extreme of denunciation. She put in a few objections which provoked Gwen to lump her along with the Captain as one of the enemy. They were essentially the same kind, she

84

insisted: conventional because they were afraid of anything different, anything new. To her and the Captain anyone who conformed was good, anyone who didn't bad.

This made Katharine angry herself. Partly because it was untrue and anyway, as usual with Gwen, a ridiculous oversimplification of what even the Captain believed; partly because she was afraid that there might be just a grain of truth in it somewhere; and partly because Gwen, by so furiously and exclusively championing Hugo, was appropriating him to herself. This too was a familiar process. The wrangling became hotter and ended in Gwen slamming out of Katharine's bedroom and stumping noisily away to her own.

Her guilt over having supported, even though in reaction to Gwen, some small part of the Captain's case, was made worse by Hugo's present behaviour. He seemed, on the second encounter, so pleasant and so genuinely pleased to see them. Smooth and tricky, the Captain had said – but he was not at all like that. He had been baking bread before they arrived – he bought wholemeal flour by the sack and made it into dough and let it rise under muslin on racks above the oven – and from one of the loaves he cut them thick warm slices into which the butter melted. It tasted marvellous.

He chatted as he drew, asking questions about the people at the House. Had they mentioned seeing him to Miss Hunston? Gwen said,

'No. We did to the Captain, though.'

'Ah, the Captain. How is the old boy? Still working like a horse, I suppose.'

"The row you had with him," Gwen asked, "– what was it about?"

"We didn't really have a row. Just a – shall we say, a growing lack of sympathy? I used to pull his leg a little, and it turned out our senses of humour were not compatible."

"When was this?" Katharine asked.

"I don't remember." He smiled at her. "What is time when you live in a cottage in the wilderness? My clocks are the flowers and trees, the birds. It's a quarter past summer now. About seven or eight weeks ago, I suppose. Though you could say the estrangement was coming on before that."

Gwen said, "Do you really think he *is* a Captain, and that he fought in the Desert?"

"What makes you ask?"

"Well, the way he talks."

Hugo looked at her acutely. "Don't tell me you're an accent snob."

"No, of course not. But . . ."

"Or that you think only people who speak like BBC announcers are ever given the Queen's commission."

Gwen for once looked helpless; taken aback by the sharpness and unexpectedness of Hugo's response. Katharine said,

"It's more the things he says than the way he says them. This death-or-glory stuff." She tried mimicking him though Gwen would have done it better: "' The Hun was a clean fighter, same as us;" Hugo laughed but went on drawing. "And about going from Alamein to Algiers which the Eighth Army didn't do. And surely people who were Captains in the army don't call themselves Captain afterwards."

"Very shrewd," Hugo said. "You are an observant young woman – I must remember that. What *you* must remember is that people who are actually quite genuine sometimes overplay their roles. The old tar gets absurdly nautical, shivering his timbers and all that jazz, and the old sweat – old soldier, that is – uses terms he's picked up from fifth-rate journalists. And perhaps stretches the facts a bit in the way those jokers do. He certainly didn't fight his way from Alamein to Algiers, but that doesn't mean he didn't fight at Alamein. And as for calling himself Captain, I agree a pukka-sahib old-school-tie ex-officer wouldn't, but the Captain's not one of those and doesn't claim to be. He calls himself Captain because he's proud of the one big achievement of his life, and has good right to be."

"Do you know all this," Gwen asked, "or are you just guessing?"

She was disappointed that Hugo should defend the Captain instead of joining in her attack on him. Katharine was as much impressed. It showed just how far off the mark the Captain's judgement of Hugo had been. If he were tricky and untrustworthy he would scarcely have spoken up like this for a man he knew disliked him.

Hugo said, "Principally I'm showing you that it's unwise to jump to conclusions – that there's often an alternative and better explanation of the facts. But as it happens, I *do* know. The Captain was in the Eighth Army, in the Desert, and he was promoted in the field, from Sergeant to full Lieutenant. It was the sort of thing that happened sometimes when there were heavy casualties among officers and no time to bring in replacements. I suppose he got his third pip later as a routine, but he would be unlikely to get any further than that. I shouldn't think he ever felt much at ease in an Officer's Mess."

Gwen said, "Did he tell you that – about being promoted on the field of battle?"

Hugo said benignly, "We *are* suspicious, aren't we? No, it was Mrs Castle. And to forestall the obvious next question, she had seen evidence – a newspaper cutting he carries in his wallet as a souvenir of past greatness. He showed it to her one day when he was a little bit in his cups."

"If he was an officer," Gwen said, "I still don't see why he sticks in a job like that. I mean, mostly he's a kind of odd-job man."

"He wasn't the kind of officer who would be offered a seat on a Board of Directors or a big executive post in industry. But there is a little more to it. I gather both he and Mrs Castle have expectations."

"Expectations of what?"

"Of your aunt's estate. Now don't look worried. She's not going to leave the entire family fortune to her faithful servitors. But a few thousand, say, which sounds a lot to someone like me – or to the Captain. It represents security for his old age. Miss Hunston, like many rich people, is more easily reconciled to paying out after she's dead than while she's still alive. And since, I am sure, she is a woman of her word, Mrs Castle and the Captain are quite happy to make do with a pittance now, and to live this primitive life at the back of beyond."

"They might die before she does," Sarah said.

Hugo laughed. "Yes. That would be tough luck, wouldn't it? But she is older than they are, and in poor health. Weak heart, isn't it?"

Katharine said, "I suppose you learnt all this from Mrs Castle?"

"Well, yes. I wouldn't say the Captain was all that confiding to me."

"They get the legacy providing they're still in Aunt Marion's employment when she dies – is that it?"

"I imagine so."

"And therefore they have to do as she says. Not just in the ordinary way of people working for other people, but

88

having to be careful all the time not to offend her. Because it's not just next week's wages at stake, but thousands of pounds."

"Something of the sort." Hugo looked at her curiously over the top of his sketching board. "You seem to take that seriously."

Katharine remembered her aunt talking about her childhood, and the rabbit and the pennies. 'One learnt the value of money.' She said,

"It's disgusting."

"Not if all concerned are happy."

"That makes no difference. In fact, it makes it worse."

"You're a Puritan," Hugo said.

"No, I'm not."

"In the best sense of the word. You set high standards, for yourself and other people. Very commendable, but it can also be uncomfortable."

"*I'm* a bit uncomfortable," Gwen said. She was obviously not relishing the turn the conversation had taken. "Can we move yet?"

"Yes, of course," Hugo said. "It's time for a break. I wasn't thinking."

Gwen relaxed in an enormous extrovert wriggle. Hugo said,

"Sorry the chairs are so hard. I've only got the one cushion, and I thought Sarah's knees were first priority."

Gwen stood up and rubbed the top of her leg. She said,

"We could do with a couple of those armchairs from the tower room."

Hugo was still filling in his sketch. He said,

"The tower at the House? Is it furnished, then? I assumed it was derelict."

Gwen said, "Oh, no! the bottom bit's a mess but the top's super. It's our special place."

Mine originally, Katharine thought. Gwen was appropriating again. She chattered on, about their discovering the gas-fire still worked, about the things they had found there – the miniature paintings, tarnished silver in the sideboard, the chest full of old documents.

Hugo said, "Sounds fun. You can look now."

He showed them the sketch, with their faces recognizably emerging from the pattern of lines and squiggles. Gwen and Sarah made sounds of enthusiasm. Hugo looked at Katharine.

"It's only a rough, of course. How do you like it?"

She was always embarrassed, alarmed almost, by photographs of herself, and the sketch had the same effect. She said,

"It's very good."

"No, it's not," Hugo said, "but it's the best I can do. Rembrandt need fear no competition from me. Now, how about trying my home-made nettle beer? I really am good at that."

6

Katharine asked: "Why do you limp?"

It was not a question she would have put in real life; it was too blunt, too careless of the other person's sensitivity. But she knew she was asleep and dreaming, and in the dream it seemed natural. The woman said:

"I had an accident, a fall. A long time ago."

"Did it hurt a lot?"

"It's hard to remember. It was so long ago."

"I've always been frightened of being hurt like that – breaking a leg or something."

This was true, the expression of a recurrent secret fear. It too she would not normally have revealed, to anyone. The woman smiled, with a small shake of her head.

"You need not be."

In the dream she was clearer and more substantial. The grey in which she was dressed was of satin, and had a brocaded pattern of small roses, lighter in shade than the rest of the material. Objects behind her did not show through. Katharine could see her face, marked by lines of age and perhaps of sadness. But the sadness, if it had once existed, was over. Her look was serene and happy; strong. When she said there was no need for fear, Katharine felt the fear itself unwind its hold and go.

They were walking through the house together. There

was no sign or sound of any other person, and an awareness, beyond the senses, that no one else was here: they
were quite alone.

"I'm Katharine Morris. I'm on a visit to my aunt, with
my two sisters."

It seemed appropriate to introduce herself, and yet unnecessary. The woman nodded, and said "Yes". Katharine
wondered where Gwen and Sarah had got to and then
thought how silly that was – she was dreaming and there
was no particular reason why they should be with her in
the dream.

Their footsteps echoed slightly. When they passed
windows she did not look out but honey-coloured light
seemed to flood in and wrap round them both. She was
at ease, as she could not recall having been with another
person; not even Sarah, or Gwen in her good moods.
There was no need to say anything, but at the same time
speaking would not spoil it. She said,

"You lived here, too, didn't you?"

"Most of my life," the woman said.

"And you love the house."

"Yes," the woman said, "as you do."

Hearing the words she knew them to be true. She loved
this house.

"Where are those other two?" Mrs Castle asked.
"Slipped off again, I suppose. Well, they're not all that
much help when they are here."

Gwen and Sarah had disappeared after bringing the last
lot of washing in from the line outside. They were probably,
the weather being still raw with more rain threatening,
up in the tower room. Katharine thought of saying, in
answer to the criticism, that after all it was supposed to be
a holiday, but decided it was not worth it. A blanket had

been placed over the big kitchen table and she was ironing at one end, Mrs Castle at the other. The irons were long narrow affairs of solid metal, which were heated by being stood on end with their bases up against the opened front of the stove. They were awkward and tiring to use, but she struggled on, determined not to show weakness.

Mrs Castle said, "You're worth half a dozen of the pair of them put together. I know you're the eldest, but it's not that. Funny how it happens. My sister was a bit like your Gwen. She was found a place with a good family but she just wouldn't settle to service. She went into Woolworth's instead. That was when they first started up. Nothing over sixpence. A cheap nasty place, serving nasty common people; but she'd rather do that than roll her sleeves up and get down to real work. I don't know . . . I suppose such as you and me are fools not to take things easy like the rest do. But I wouldn't be like them for all the jewels in Her Majesty's crown. I wouldn't, I tell you."

The remarks about Gwen and Sarah had been bad enough and the praise of herself worse; but being bracketed with Mrs Castle – "such as you and me" – was unbearable. To change the subject she asked about Hugo. He had said he had a long-standing distant connection with Aunt Marion: did Mrs Castle have any idea what it was?

"He's the son of an old friend of hers," Mrs Castle said. "She told me about it not long after he came here and she let him have the gatehouse cottage. Some girl she had known at school, or something, who'd married unhappily and died young. That was why she let him go and live there, because of remembering this friend. She's got her sentimental side, has your aunt."

In silence Katharine ironed the leg of Gwen's trousers. Mrs Castle took her own iron to the stove and fetched another. Running it up and down past her cheek, she said,

"Not that I can understand why a man, and youngish too, would be wanting to live on his own in a place like that, with no one else in sight or sound."

"He's an artist," Katharine said.

"That I know. He showed me one of his pictures, but I wouldn't know if it was good, bad or indifferent. He offered to do one of me for ten pounds and it would be a nest-egg for my old age – worth thousands once he was famous. Famous!"

One of Hugo's little jokes, Katharine thought, and wasted on someone with as small a sense of humour as Mrs Castle. Stringing it along herself, she said,

"Perhaps he will be. Famous, that is."

"Queerer things have happened, I suppose. But if he's an artist, why isn't he in one of those Art Schools in London or Paris or somewhere?"

"They're for people who are still learning, surely."

"Well, and if he isn't still learning, he ought to be taking it more seriously – not living in a hut and selling paintings for a pound or two in some back street in Manpool. You don't get anywhere by sitting around and frittering your life away."

Katharine concentrated on a blouse, her own. The frill would have been tricky enough with a proper iron and was just about impossible with the monster she was using. Her wrist and arm ached from the strain. After a minute or so of silence, Mrs Castle said,

"Mind you, I liked him well enough. He's got nice manners, and he's thoughtful. If more men were like him, life would be pleasanter for women."

"That wasn't the way the Captain felt, I gather."

"Oh, the Captain! They were cat and dog, as you might expect. The Captain couldn't stand him: that beard, and

94

his clothes, and his way of talking. And being an artist, of course. His nice manners didn't do him any good with the Captain, either. You'll find, acushla, that there's two kinds of men. One kind knows what to say to women, nice things, things that put you at your ease; and the other doesn't. The ones that don't can never understand the ones that do. He used to hear me talking to Hugo here in the kitchen, laughing with him maybe, and he'd come in like a bear with a sore head." She added complacently, "Just jealousy, that's all."

The idea of Mrs Castle as an object of rivalry between Hugo and the Captain was so funny that Katharine's hand shook and she nearly ruined the blouse. She said hastily,

"Didn't Aunt Marion say anything when the Captain and Hugo had their big row?"

"I don't suppose she knew. I certainly wouldn't tell her. I wouldn't be distressing her with that sort of thing, and her heart not strong at all."

"But didn't she make any comment about Hugo not coming any more?"

"It wasn't as though she knew he'd *been* coming. He didn't get into the House – well, no further than this kitchen."

"Why was that?"

"Oh, I suppose he'd have been glad enough to get in, and chat to her half the day the way he would with me. But I think she made it plain she wasn't having any of it."

"But if he was the son of an old friend?"

"Well, it was because of that she let him have the cottage. But she wasn't going to have him getting ideas of there being anything more to come. She's very scrupulous is Miss Hunston, in that sort of thing."

Katharine said, "Yes, I see."

95

It was presumably the same reasoning which had prompted her to keep her contacts with the Morris family to the barest minimum, until after she broke with her Rhodesian nephew.

Mrs Castle looked at her with a knowing smile.

"She's very taken with you. I was telling her only this morning what a help you were, and she looked as pleased as if I'd been talking about her own daughter."

Katharine went on ironing and did not reply.

Sarah asked, "But when are you going to start *painting*, Hugo?"

Hugo looked at them over his sketch-pad.

"Gwen, turn your head just a touch to the right, will you? Beg your pardon, I meant left. My right. That's it. When am I going to start painting? You mean, sloshing paint on a canvas. I don't know. When I get the bare bones lined up as they ought to be, and I've not done that yet."

"But will you have time to finish it? We're only here another three weeks."

"It's the preliminaries that take up most of the time," Hugo said. "Once the structure's right it's an easy run."

He looked at the pad and shook his head.

"We've quite a way to go yet, though. I need a break and so do you, I imagine. Who's for nettle beer?"

They took their mugs outside and sat on the bench. The green and yellow splotches, Hugo had told them, had been painted on to produce an effect of sunlight falling through branches: it cheered him up, he said, when the sun was not shining. But it was shining today, warm on their arms and faces, superimposing its own pattern of light and shade on the painted one.

Hugo said, "I feel restless. Can't settle to things."

Gwen said, "I feel a bit like that."

"I meant to pick beans this morning but I haven't got round to it." He pointed to the row of stakes halfway down the cultivated patch, supporting bean plants hung with long green pods. "Suppose you wouldn't be a honey and pull me a pound or two?"

"Where's the basket?" Gwen asked.

"Behind the door."

Sarah was sitting on the ground beside the seat. Hugo said,

"I've got a second crop of strawberries down at the end, I find. Might be enough for us all to have a mouthful." He ruffled Sarah's hair. "And an extra mouthful for the picker if no one's looking. Take the colander – it's hanging over the sink."

Katharine asked, "What's my job?"

"Sitting beside me in the sun."

She had a feeling that there was something behind the various requests, that for some reason he wanted her on her own. She felt flattered – usually he paid more attention to Gwen – but a little uneasy. She watched the other two go down the garden. When they were out of earshot Hugo said, his voice lower than usual,

"I want to talk to you, Kate."

She did not say anything. He went on,

"You're older than the others. And you understand things better. I should think you know a bit more about discretion, too."

He paused, waiting for her to say something but she did not. He said,

"I told you I knew your aunt before I came here. Has anything been said about that – about how I came to know her?"

"Mrs Castle said you were the son of an old friend of hers."

"And your aunt?"

"I haven't mentioned you to her."

"It's complicated," Hugo said, "and it goes back a long way. My grandfather was in business with her father at one time. They split up, and my grandfather didn't do so well on his own. He did badly, in fact, very badly. He died before I was born and there was practically nothing to leave to my mother. He'd become very eccentric the last few years. He bought useless shares in things like abandoned gold mines. He left a terrible clutter behind him."

Gwen in the distance waved to them, flourishing a bean of enormous length. Hugo said,

"To cut a long story short, when my mother died herself eighteen months ago I had to sort her things out. There were a lot of grandfather's papers which she had never looked at. I went through them. I found a letter which he must have written to her shortly before he died, but never sent. I know she said his memory had gone and he used to forget what he was doing, would put things down and not be able to find them. Anyway, there was one bit which was interesting. He mentioned some land he'd bought from old Hunston years before. He said he'd been moving about a lot at the time – he went to America for a couple of years – and he'd left all the documents in Hunston's care: deeds, transfer documents, that sort of thing. She was to get in touch with Hunston and ask him for them.

"The land was here, on this estate. He'd bought it because although they were no longer in business together they were still friends, and I suppose it struck them both as a good idea to have him build a house not far from Hunston. He imagined he'd be able to retire in a few years and live in luxury. The letter said there was five acres of land and gave a good idea where it is. It runs along the outside of the wall between here and the other gate. It's waste land now, but it's not far from a new dormitory suburb for Manpool that's being planned. I've talked to an estate agent and he's told me it could fetch a couple of thousand pounds, maybe more."

Katharine said, "Did you speak to my aunt about it?"

"That was why I got in touch with her. I showed her the letter. She said it meant nothing – my grandfather was crazy and had delusions. Well, he was eccentric as I've said but this letter read very sanely to me. It had all sorts of details about the land. She said anyone could say land belonged to him. There had to be legal proof of ownership. That's quite right, of course. I asked her if she would have a look for the documents he'd said her father was holding. She said there was no point in doing that: everything was kept at her solicitor's and they would have told her if there had been anything of the sort.

"I explained to her why the money would be so useful – I want to go to Italy and paint. That was when she told me I could have the use of this cottage. It was better than nothing, so I thanked her and accepted. But I've been thinking over what Gwen was saying the other day – particularly about that old chest in the tower-room which is full of documents. I don't suppose any of it has been looked at for years. What I want just could be in there."

Katharine said, "You could ask her to let you have a look."

"I could, but she might not agree. She's a funny old girl in some ways. And . . ." He hesitated for a moment. "I get the impression she's, well, a bit of a miser. It may sound terrible, but I couldn't be sure she wouldn't put me off with an excuse and have a look herself first. And if she found the documents she might still decide not to give them to me. In fact, she might destroy them."

Katharine did not believe that, but it was certainly true that Aunt Marion was a bit of a miser and hated parting with anything. She would hate the thought of losing land most of all probably, even though it was on the far side of the wall. So she could understand Hugo's suspicions. She said,

"Would you like me to look in the chest for you?"

"Well . . ." He paused. "Not really, Kate. The way these legal things are done I'm not sure you would recognize the right thing if you saw it. I've had a bit of experience – I worked in a solicitor's office once – and I know how incomprehensible lawyer's jargon is to a lay person. And then even if the deeds themselves aren't there, one might find something else which would help, a clue of some kind. But again you'd have to know what you were looking for."

"Then what . . . ?"

"If I could get in there myself and have a rummage through – I could do it in half an hour, probably less. But naturally I don't want to actually break in. That's burglary and a felony. If anything went wrong – the Captain caught me, say – I'd go to prison. For a long time, too. But it's not burglary if you walk in through an open door. I know Mrs Castle locks and bars everything at night. But if you could slip down afterwards and open the back door . . . Any other doors there are, too, between the kitchen and the tower-room."

Katharine said slowly, "The doors inside aren't locked."

"And you'd have to tell me just how to get to the tower-room. I've only been in the main part of the house."

She tried to think clearly. It was her aunt's house. She was a guest and had no possible right to open a door at night to let someone in without her aunt's knowledge. But Hugo was only looking for something which, if it were

there, he was fully entitled to have. It might not exist –
very likely Aunt Marion had been right in saying that his
grandfather was crazy and had made up the whole thing –
and in that case there was no harm done. Hugo would just
have to accept his disappointment. On the other hand if
there were proof it was horribly unfair to Hugo that it
should be kept hidden.

Hugo said, "Will you?" His eyes fixed on her. The
appeal was direct. "If I could manage to get abroad even
for a year it could make all the difference. My kind of
painting needs more colour than one gets from these grey
English skies."

Deep blue at the moment, with the sunlit trees sharply
etched against it, but she knew what he meant. She said,
"I'd like to think about it."

"No." He took her hand, his fingers warm and firm
without crushing. "Don't do that. Never think about it if
someone asks you to help them. Say yes or no, but say it
right away."

"Well . . ."

"I realize it's a lot to ask. I suppose I'm grabbing at
something which could eventually be a part of your
inheritance."

She flushed and saw him watching her. Almost angrily,
she said,

"I'll do it."

He said quietly, "I was sure you wouldn't let me down.
The back door, then, tonight?"

"Tonight?"

She was shocked by the suddenness of it. Hugo said,
"Sooner the better."

"I could stay up, and let you in myself."

"No, don't. I don't want you to get involved in case
something goes wrong. Just unlcock the door, slip the

bolts, and go back to bed. And draw me a map of the route from the back door to the tower-room. Here's paper and pencil."

She drew it quickly and badly. She said,

"It's not very good, I'm afraid."

"It's fine." He took the sketch and put it in his pocket. "The gatherers are returning, I see. Look, I wouldn't say anything to them about this."

"Of course not."

He grinned at her. "If it comes off, the first picture I paint in Italy is yours. And I'll send you a ticket to my exhibition at the Wildenstein. I'll dedicate the exhibition to you, if you like."

"No, I'd rather not."

He squeezed her hand. "Good old Kate."

Katharine felt restless and on edge for the remainder of the day. She got irritated with Gwen, who was in one of her ebullient moods. Gwen also talked interminably about Hugo: what a super person he was, how marvellous he was at doing things, his terrific sense of humour . . .

Katharine said, "For God's sake! We realize you're besotted, but do let's have a rest from Hugo."

"Someone," Gwen announced, "feels she has not been getting enough attention. But you don't have to be quite so obvious about it."

Her private knowledge of how much more seriously Hugo took her than he did Gwen ought to have allowed her to rise superior to that. Instead she found her annoyance increasing. She said,

"Going to the cinema a few times with Spotty Robin and holding hands at the back of the stalls doesn't exactly qualify you as a *femme fatale*. Do try to remember that to someone of Hugo's age you're just a grubby little schoolgirl. And I mean grubby. If he noticed anything about you today, it would be that your fingernails badly need cleaning."

Gwen looked at her hands and saw this was true. It made her furiously angry; she was normally very scrupulous about details like that and probably spent too much time attending to them. She snapped back sharply and they bickered until they were interrupted by Mrs Castle's gong calling them to tea.

During tea there was a strained silence. Katharine felt irritated with herself and Gwen, and increasingly with Sarah who was showing signs of a relapse into bad table manners. There was no one thing which was outrageous until near the end, when Sarah reached over grossly and without excuse to grab the last cake on the tray. They were chocolate-iced and she had already had two. Mrs Castle, who had popped in to have a cup of tea with them, gave her a significant look as she went out to the kitchen. Katharine, as the door closed, let fly with a blistering tirade, to which Sarah responded first with surprise and then with hurt indignation.

Gwen said, "Oh, never mind her, Sarah! She's impossible today. Just don't pay any attention."

Since Gwen was the most constant and venomous critic of Sarah's behaviour at table, this was galling. The two of them got up together and left, Gwen working hard at the unaccustomed role of ally and comforter to her younger sister. Katharine stared, hard-eyed and feeling herself almost trembling with nerves, at the table for some minutes before she was able to collect herself together and make a start at clearing.

She got away as soon as she could from Mrs Castle, whose chatter she found more than usually trying. She went out into the garden, alternately trying to think and not to think.

The general atmosphere of dilapidation was even more apparent here than in the house. The walks were full of holes and the hedges badly clipped. Most of the colour in the flower-beds came from marigolds, which her father insisted were not flowers at all but weeds and which in places were running riot. She came across a few weakly flowering rose trees, one of which, a grafted standard, had reverted to the briar. There was a long rectangular stone trough, about ten feet by four, which had obviously been a fishpond at one time – the nozzle of a broken fountain jutted up in the centre – but had been filled with boulders and earth and converted into a rockery. Not a very good one: there were a few clumps of saxifrage and house-leek, very little else. The lawns like the hedges had been cut, but roughly; and plantains had taken a stranglehold on them.

She thought of what it might have been like in the old days, kept in immaculate trim by the gardeners: two, Mrs Castle had told her, plus a couple of boys. The golden glimmer of fish leaping in the pond at dusk, the scent of a thousand roses, women in silk dresses walking over smoothly perfect lawns ... You could not call time back but surely if Aunt Marion were as rich as everyone seemed to think it should be possible to look after the place a little better than this. It was too much to expect the Captain to do it all, and in spare moments snatched from his other jobs. She felt a quick surge of resentment against her aunt for her miserliness. She hoped Hugo found his document and took the patch of land away from her; what she had she neglected, after all.

The high box hedge, shorn somewhat at the sides but unchecked at the top, which separated this part from the kitchen garden had a gap at the end where an unpainted wooden gate hung derelict from a single hinge. She was almost here when the Captain appeared from the other side. She would have turned away if he had not been so close; as it was she had to wait for him to come up.

"Fine evening," he said. He drew breath in deeply and exhaled with a gusty sigh. "And a good day tomorrow, I would say."

The sun had set but the western sky was rose, streaked with gold where a few high clouds were lit from beyond the horizon. Katharine nodded. The Captain said,

"I always like a garden best just after the sun's gone down. The scent of the day's still there and there's the smell of the night along with it. Everything's peaceful."

He was in a talkative mood. She had to listen to him but at least did not have to make much response. He got on to the war again though in more reflective fashion. He talked about the different swifter sunsets, the coolness of evening after the burning aridness of the African day. A place they were stationed at after the campaign, near a town called Sfax, with a beach of miles and miles of white sand where they bathed in the moonlight. The sea all warm and still and silver. And melon fields close up to the beach with Arab boys guarding them, sitting there along with their dogs . . .

He stopped and looked at her. "You're a grave one at times."

"I'm sorry. I . . ."

The Captain shook his head. "I like it. When you're grave, with those two little wrinkles above your eyes – you remind me of my daughter."

"Your daughter?"

Her surprise probably showed; Mrs Castle had said the

Captain was unmarried, not the marrying kind of man. He said,

"It's a long time since I've seen her." He was silent and she did not know what to say. Then he went on, "That beach at Sfax. One reason I remember it so well is that I got the letter there. From my wife. I thought it was going to be a reply to my letter, telling her I'd been made up to an officer, and I opened it quick, thinking how pleased she would be. It wasn't, though. She hadn't had my letter then. It was to tell me there was this other man – had been for a year – an American, and he was being posted back to America and she was going to go with him. And take Linda. She was a bit younger than you. Nearly thirteen. I'd been in Sfax that day, trying to find something for her birthday."

Katharine said, "I'm sorry."

He shook his head. "You get over things. I did see Linda again, once. It was a few years after the war. She came over from America and looked me up. I didn't even know she had my address. She was eighteen, grown up and pretty. And an American. She talked a bit like Doris Day. She wanted to stay and look after me. She felt bad about having gone away, with me overseas, though of course it was nothing to do with her. But she could never bear to do anything shabby, anything underhand, and that's the way it had seemed to her."

"What did you say to her?"

"What could I say? She was really happy where she was. Used to a different sort of life. And fond of her step-father. I told her to go back – I was set in my ways and better on my own. She wrote to me and I didn't write back. It wouldn't have done any good. But I was glad she'd come to see me, that she was still straight, the way I'd known her, wanting to do the right thing."

They walked towards the house in silence. He said before they parted,

"It's a long time ago and I don't talk about it."

She nodded. "I understand, Captain."

"But you remind me of her."

She felt depressed, not only on account of the Captain but in the recollection of what she had committed herself to. She could imagine what the Captain would think of her if he knew. She would certainly not remind him of his daughter who could never bear to do anything shabby or underhand. He would regard this as shabby, all right; mean and unjustifiable whatever the excuse.

She had an idea suddenly, so blindingly obvious that she could not think why it had not occurred to her before. Hugo had said there was no point in her searching the chest for what he wanted because she would not recognize it, or might miss something which offered a clue. But the papers and documents she had seen, although admittedly she had not examined them very closely, had given the impression of being a couple of hundred years old at least. Hugo was talking about a transaction that had taken place not all that long before he was born – certainly in this century. If there were nothing there as recent as that . . .

It was growing dark and although the gas-fire in the tower-room had worked she doubted if the gas-lights would. She went to her room and got the torch they had brought with them from home. Then she hurried downstairs and through the conservatory to the tower. The stairs creaked horribly beneath her feet and she had a moment's panic about the empty room above. But it was quiet and peaceful and brighter than she had expected, the wide windows drawing in the full western light of the sky.

She opened the chest and, kneeling beside it, ruffled quickly through its contents.

Not everything was dated, but of those that were not plainly very old – written with "f" for "s" in ink fading from the paper – the latest date was 1857. All the documents must have been old in Aunt Marion's father's time. There was nothing which could have anything to do with what Hugo was looking for. She closed the chest and went to sit by the window. If she had known earlier she could have gone to the cottage and told him. It was quarter to ten by her watch. Mrs Castle locked up punctually at ten so that there was no time for that now even if she had fancied the trek through the woods with night coming on fast.

She must keep her promise of opening up; otherwise Hugo would be left standing out there in the middle of the night. She toyed with the notion of writing a note and pinning it on the door where he would see it, but decided on reflection that she could not be sure that the Captain, who sometimes went out for a late stroll, would not see it too. There was only one solution, she saw: she must stay down in the kitchen and tell him herself, when he came in.

The preliminaries went very well. She waited till the house was quiet and crept downstairs. She lit the gas-light in the kitchen but turned it low. She knew now where Mrs Castle kept the back-door key – on a nail inside the larder – and she undid the lock and drew both sets of bolts. Then she curled up in Mrs Castle's kitchen chair and settled herself to wait. She thought of Hugo. It would be a disappointment for him but there was no help for that. Was it all that important, anyway, for him to go and paint in Italy? She did not know enough about painting – did not really know anything, in fact – to be able to judge. It might be possible to help by tackling Aunt Marion on his behalf. If Aunt Marion were made to realize that the land really was Hugo's by right, Katharine was sure she would not try to keep it. She might be mean, but she was honest. And if she had it in mind to leave everything to Daddy when she died . . .

Her mind drifted from Hugo to the woman in grey. The thought was a peaceful one, attractive rather than alarming. She had not spoken of her to anyone. This was the sort of time, in the still of night, when she might see her again. Her eyelids had closed and she opened them, half expecting to see the figure before her. But there was nothing. She wondered how long it was since the woman had lived in the house. It had been in dream that she had talked of living here most of her life; but in a strange way the dream was real, as real as Hugo or Aunt Marion or Gwen's bad temper, the things in it beyond any possible doubt or query.

When she opened her eyes again it was in jerking into wakefulness from sleep that had left her stiff and cramped. The gas-light still burned, but the window's square was beginning to brighten. It must be early morning. Perhaps Hugo had decided against coming. Then she realized something else. A blanket, the one Mrs Castle used for ironing and kept on a shelf over the stove, had been draped over her. Hugo must have done that, finding her asleep when he crept in. Then had he gone away again, too, without waking her?

He might not have done, she thought as her mind cleared of sleep. He might be in the tower-room at this moment, looking through the papers in the chest.

She took the torch and went quickly through the house. Climbing the stairs produced the usual protesting groans of wood. She called out, loud enough to be heard in the top room, "All right, Hugo – it's me, Katharine." Then she was up and could see the room was empty.

She saw something else as the beam of her torch tracked round the walls. The paintings of the ships were still in place but the miniatures had gone, their absence emphasized by the darker patches of wallpaper where they had hung. She stood staring for a moment before she understood. Then she felt sick and dizzy, and had to put her hand on the balustrade or she might have fallen.

7

Gwen slept as she always did with the bedclothes pulled tightly round her, enclosing her in a sort of cocoon. She did not respond to Katharine's first touch but came blinkingly awake on a more vigorous shaking.

She said, "What . . . Kate? What's the matter? What time is it?" She sat up in the grey dawn light. "It's middle of the night still."

Katharine said, "I've got to talk to you."

"Talk? What about? Have you had a nightmare or something?"

"It's Hugo."

"What about him? *Hugo?* What on earth are you raving about?"

"He's stolen things from the tower-room. The miniatures. And the silver."

Gwen halted in mid-yawn. "You've been dreaming. How could he?"

"Because I've just come from there."

Katharine felt her voice quiver and almost break. Gwen looked at her, taking her seriously at last. She said,

"But what were you doing in the tower-room? And what makes you think it's Hugo?"

She took a breath and plunged in, telling Gwen about the conversation that had taken place while the other two were picking beans and strawberries. Gwen listened without interruption up to the point where Katharine spoke of agreeing to leave the back door open for him. Then she said,

"Oh, you idiot! But *why*?"

She could not explain. The thing that had really tipped the balance, Hugo's remark about the possibility of their inheriting from Aunt Marion, was too ridiculous to tell. She said,

"I just didn't imagine . . . I thought he was all right."

"Hugo?"

The scorn in Gwen's voice helped pull her together. She said,

"You wouldn't have thought any differently. You were always on about how marvellous he was."

"Of course, he was marvellous! Absolutely super. But that doesn't mean I would trust him. You are an innocent, aren't you? I mean, surely you know that as far as men are concerned being super has nothing to do with being reliable?"

It was an unpleasant change to have Gwen ticking her off for being immature. And there was really not much she could do except take it. She said,

"It was convincing because it was so complicated. He must have spent hours thinking it out. All those details. And why should he do something so stupid. He knows he'll go to prison if he gets caught."

Gwen said, "I thought he was listening pretty closely when I was talking about the things in the tower-room. He asked what kind of dress the people in the miniature paintings were wearing, and I said different kinds but a couple sort of Elizabethan. Remember? So they had to be old, and I suppose he might know if they would be valuable, being a painter himself. Fairly easy to carry, too.

And silver's always likely to be worth a bit, isn't it? I suppose he'd got tired of living in the cottage, painting, and thought he'd take some loot with him when he bunked."

"But he's bound to get caught."

"He may not be."

"I was asleep in the kitchen. He even put a blanket over me. If I'd wakened . . ."

"He'd have told you some story. He'll probably be in London by midday. And then off round to some shady picture dealer."

The remark – 'He'd have told you some story' – hurt, too. But there were more important considerations than wounded pride. Gwen's speculations on Hugo's next moves reminded her that the situation was urgent. She said,

"Aunt Marion."

"What about her?"

"I must tell her."

"She'll be furious." Gwen twisted her face in a grimace of horror and alarm. "How can you? I mean, *how*? Apart from letting him in, there's your reason for doing it. He'd as good as said Aunt Marion was cheating him, and you believed it."

"I didn't believe it. I thought . . ."

"It's going to look to her as though you believed it. What else? You *can't* tell her that."

"I've got to." Katharine felt herself going weak at the prospect. "I must."

"No, wait!" Gwen brought her knees up and propped elbows on them. "Let's think a bit. Until we went there no one had been in the tower-room for ages. Years. Not even Mrs Castle. Remember how thick the dust was everywhere."

"Yes, but . . ."

"And no one knows we've been up there."

This also was true. It had been mentioned to Hugo, but they had kept quiet as far as Aunt Marion and Mrs Castle were concerned; not entirely through fear of being prohibited from using it. There was also the attraction of keeping it as a secret place. Katharine thought again of Hugo rifling its contents and shivered with shame and anger.

Gwen said, "Aunt Marion doesn't bother about her things even in the rest of the house. She may not look in the tower-room for years, not ever, maybe. And if she does, or Mrs Castle goes up there, they won't know when the stuff was taken, will they? It could have been any time. The only thing is, we'd better stop using it ourselves, just in case."

Katharine said, "I can't do that."

"Why not?"

She shook her head. "I can't."

"Well, you can't go and tell Aunt Marion what a nit you've been – and that you believed Hugo when he said she was a crook."

"I suppose Hugo . . ."

"What?"

"May have thought I wouldn't dare tell her – that I'd do as you say and keep quiet about it."

"He might."

"I must tell her."

She turned away from the bed. Gwen cried,

"You don't mean right now!"

"Yes."

"And wake her up to tell her? You can leave it till later, at least. Think about it a bit first. You could say you went up there after breakfast and found out. That's if you really have to say anything. I honestly think . . ."

Katharine said, "If she rings the police right away there will be more chance of catching him. They can check the roads and railway stations."

"But does it matter whether or not they catch him?"

She said firmly, "Yes, it does."

"It's not as though the things he took are important to her. She never looks at them."

"That's not the point."

Gwen appeared to realize her mind was made up. She shrugged. "It's your funeral." She hesitated. "Do you want me to come with you?"

Katharine realized she had committed herself and felt desperately weak again. She said,

"No. That's all right."

"Don't go yet," Gwen said. "At least think up some better story for letting him in. You don't have to make it look as black as all that."

"I must."

Gwen groaned. "If you say so. Come back and tell me what happened."

"If you aren't asleep."

"I won't be." She lay down and dragged the bedclothes round her. "Poor you."

Katharine stared at the closed door of Aunt Marion's bedroom. The corridor was dimly lit by the gas lamps, here and at the top of the stairs, which were kept on low all night. It was just after five o'clock. She could hear birds in the distance, a whistling chatter punctuated by the deeper harshness of rooks. It would be easier, as Gwen had said, to wait until she woke up naturally – a lot easier.

She clenched her fists, digging her nails sharply into her hands, and rapped on the door. It sounded much too loud; demanding, almost impudent. Her aunt's voice called from inside,

"Who is it? Mrs Castle?"

"It's me. Katharine. Can I come in?"

"Yes, of course. But in heaven's name what's the matter?"

She opened the door and went in. The room was stuffy, smelling of dust and old age. Her aunt's bed was high, with tall boards of inlaid mahogany at the head and foot. Katharine said,

"I'm sorry to wake you, Aunt Marion."

"I wasn't asleep. I often waken with the birds. What is it, child? Are you ill?"

Katharine said, forcing the words out,

"Hugo's stolen things, from the tower-room. And it's my fault."

Aunt Marion's face showed no expression in the half-light. In a calm voice she said,

"You'd better tell me what it's all about. From the beginning."

Katharine did so. She stumbled in places but kept doggedly on. She did not want to look at Aunt Marion but felt she must. The thin face stared back, conveying nothing. But she was listening carefully. Interrupting Katharine's account of what she had found missing in the tower-room that morning, she said,

"And the silver? All of it?"

"Except the two trays."

"Too big, I suppose. But they are the best pieces. Go on."

There was not much more to tell. She did not mention visiting Gwen. Aunt Marion said,

"So you came to tell me right away."

"I thought I should."

"You were quite right."

"So that you can telephone the police. They might find him before he can get far."

Aunt Marion was silent for some moments. Her face was tight with what might be pain. Watching her, Katharine remembered about the bad heart. Perhaps she should have broken it to her more gently, and at a better time. If the news had shocked her badly . . . But after a time she said,

"He's a very persuasive young man. That was one of the reasons I kept him at a distance. I did not altogether trust myself where such charm is concerned. Even though I know what a thoroughly bad character he is."

There was no shock in her voice; not even surprise Katharine said,

"How did you know?"

"My dear, he has been in and out of trouble all his life. There was a business a few years ago with cheques. If it had not been for someone paying up on his behalf he would have gone to prison."

"Then why did you let him have the cottage?"

"Because his mother was a friend of mine. And he seemed more safely occupied there, painting, than he would have been roaming the country. More safely as far as his fellow citizens were concerned, certainly. I knew it would not last long. Nothing does with him. I was surprised he had not moved on before this."

"But he's taken your miniatures. And the silver."

"Yes. That is more rash than anything he has gone in for previously."

She spoke in gentle rumination. Her nightdress, Katharine noticed, was of faded blue silk and had been mended in places. She said,

"About telephoning the police. Do you want me to wake Mrs Castle?"

"There will be no need."

Did she mean she would do the telephoning herself? The telephone was in the hall, and Aunt Marion showed no sign of getting out of bed. She said,

"You yourself have not behaved in a very sensible fashion, Kitty; nor very well. It is not what I would have expected of you."

In a low voice, she said, "I know."

"But I have a feeling that you are as conscious of that as anyone – more perhaps. So it would do no good to dwell on it."

Katharine said, "I'm very sorry, Aunt Marion. For everything."

"My father used to say it is better to trust too much than too little."

But in trusting Hugo she had mistrusted Aunt Marion. She wanted to escape from her aunt's understanding and acknowledgement of that. She said,

"The police – would you like me to go and telephone them?"

"We shall not be telephoning the police."

"But if they're told now, before he gets right away . . . it's the best chance of catching him."

"He is Annabel's son. I could not be responsible for him going to prison."

"But the paintings, and the silver?" Aunt Marion gave a small shrug. "And if he goes on doing things like this?"

"If he does, I suppose eventually he will be caught and put away. But not through any act of mine." She looked at the small travelling clock on the table by her bed. "Now, go back to bed, Kitty. It is much too early to be up."

They went down to the cottage after breakfast. It was Gwen's idea. Hugo, obviously, would not be there but they might find some clue. "Clue to what?", Katharine asked, and Gwen shrugged and said, "Oh, something – anything! Anyway, we might as well do that as anything else."

She was in tearing high spirits on the way. She had said nothing more to Katharine in the way of blaming her, and had said how marvellous it was that Aunt Marion had taken it so well, but there was, Katharine felt, a strong undercurrent of satisfaction beneath the sympathy. Katharine, after all, had tended to be the superior one in the past, and Gwen could not help being a bit delighted that she had put her foot in it so calamitously now. It was only human nature, Katharine admitted, gritting her teeth.

Sarah's reaction was very different. The news had left her shocked and silent in a way that made Katharine think that perhaps she had really been fonder of Hugo than any of them, and she was still much quieter than usual. But in small ways she showed that she felt badly on Katharine's account as well. On the way to the cottage she did not respond to Gwen's jokes and clowning, and stayed close by Katharine. When they reached the cottage she put a hand out to hers, and held it.

The door was closed but only on the latch; in fact it had no lock or bolt. They went in and looked about them. The table had not been cleared and held a couple of dirty plates and a saucepan with the remains of some sort of vegetable stew. Hugo's domestic tidiness had apparently been abandoned when he decided to embark on a new life. The floor had not been swept, either. The door to the second room was open; it was even more untidy in there and the bed was unmade. In one corner was the sketchboard and some discarded sheets of drawing paper. Gwen picked one up and waved it.

"Souvenir," she said. It was the last sketch Hugo had done of them. "We'll have to make the best of it. I'm afraid we've lost our chance of hanging on the walls of the Royal Academy."

"He's left his paintings," Katharine said.

They were all there: the fantasy-abstracts and the realistic paintings of trees, the cottage, Ludmilla. It seemed to her now that the difference between the two kinds should have given her a clue to Hugo himself – to whatever deep division there was in his nature which made him unreliable and capable of folly. The whole place had a phoney look – the garish chairs, two-colour table, green-and yellow-striped dresser. It was Hugo's charm that had made it colourful and exciting. Without that it seemed cheap and trivial.

Gwen said, "He'd have had a job carrying them, especially along with his loot. And he must know they're worth nothing, anyway. Just a load of old rubbish."

Katharine saw Sarah's eyes suddenly full of tears. She asked,

"What is it, Sal?"

Sarah said, a bit choked, "The paintings."

"Comic rather than tragic, surely," Gwen said. She stood looking critically at one which had a couple of round yellow splotches set in a crimson background. "That, for instance. Too much tomato sauce on the fried eggs, it looks like."

Sarah was still looking miserable. Katharine said, "Why?"

"He was all that time here," Sarah said, "by himself. He must have thought it was something worth doing. He must have believed in the paintings then. He told lies, but

120

it wasn't all lies. Over a year here, and all winter, just by himself, just painting. And then at the end he must have thought it had all been useless, a waste. I suppose that's why he stole the things from the tower-room."

Gwen said, "He probably fooled himself as much as he fooled other people."

That was true, but Katharine felt that what Sarah had said was true also, perhaps more true. "I knew it would not last long," Aunt Marion had said. "Nothing does with him." People saw him lying and cheating, abandoning old things and going on to new. That did not necessarily mean the abandoning would be easy. For a moment she stopped feeling sorry for herself and, like Sarah, felt sorry for Hugo.

Gwen had wandered on to another canvas, the one showing the goat with a tuft of grass drooping from her mouth. She said,

"What did he do with Ludmilla, do you think? You don't suppose he took her with him, do you, like Whittington and the cat? It would make him look a bit conspicuous."

"She wasn't tethered in her usual place," Katharine said. "Perhaps he let her loose."

"We'll have to find her," Sarah said.

"Why?" Gwen asked. "She can live wild. Plenty of grass, and goats eat anything, anyway."

"She needs milking," Sarah said.

"And who," Gwen asked, "is going to do that? Can you milk a goat?"

Sarah paid no attention but ran out. She did not have far to look. The line of beanplants was shaking under a determined onslaught from the other side. Ragged holes had been torn in the green and Ludmilla's head appeared through one of them. She saw Sarah running down the garden towards her and bleated cheerfully.

Katharine's *malaise* settled into a dull depression. She did her best to conceal her feelings but everything – helping Mrs Castle, replying to things that were said, even walking about – required such an effort. She just wanted to sit down and be left alone.

People were trying to make things easy for her. Mrs Castle coaxed her to eat something at meals – she forced a little down despite having no appetite – and went on and on about how astonished she was that Hugo could have done such a thing – that she would have been taken in just as much as Katharine had been. "The trouble with people like us is that we're too trusting." She said that not once but half a dozen times. It was meant kindly and anyway Katharine felt too limp and exhausted to resent it.

The Captain, on the other hand, said nothing at all on the subject. This, especially in view of their conversation and what he had said about Katharine reminding him of his daughter, was even more unnerving. He had obviously been told of what had happened. He would have found Hugo's behaviour no surprise, merely a justification of his own suspicions, but Katharine's must have disappointed him. The mask of forbearance only slipped once, when he was engaged in relieving Ludmilla of her surplus milk. Watching him, Sarah said that Aunt Marion had said the goat could stay, at least for the time they were there on holiday, and added that she hoped she really had meant it, that Ludmilla would not be sent away.

The Captain said, "If Miss Hunston says a thing you can bank on it. She's not the person to go back on her word without good cause. Anyone ought to be able to see that – that she's straight in her dealings, all her dealings. She would never do anything shabby or underhand."

He looked up on the last sentence and Katharine saw his eyes fix on hers. She shrivelled inside. Later, on the way back to the house, he put a hand on her shoulder. She guessed he was trying to make up for what he had said, that the gesture was meant to be comforting; but it only made things worse.

In all this misery the only thing on which her mind could rest with any comfort was the woman in grey. She had no idea why this should be so; it just was. The thoughts were random at first, not directed, because her shame was deep and ingrowing, something she did not want to expose even to a ghost from the past. But despite that she got some help from them. There was a feeling, a conviction, that the figure would understand: not approve, any more than Katharine herself did, but understand, and by understanding make less hurtful.

Later she found herself searching for her deliberately, casting quick glances into corners, making excuses to go through the hall in the hope of seeing her, as she had the first time, on the stairs. She saw nothing but ordinary shadows, worn carpet, the banister rubbed bare by the long sequence of human hands. At night, then, in a dream again . . . She fastened on that. They would meet in a dream and walk through the silent house with golden sunburst coming in at the windows, and talk together. She would tell it all to her, and find comfort. There would be peace, an end to this tired nervousness which dragged her down.

She went early to bed. Aunt Marion approved of that. Katharine supposed she looked tired, having had so little sleep the night before. Drowsiness rolled over her and then, inexplicably but surely, rolled away. She lay awake for a long time. The dark darts of bats outside became more and more difficult to trace and were lost finally in the vaster darkness of the night.

At last she slept and awoke, heavy-lidded, sunlight hot on one of her arms. She thought at once of the woman in grey. Had there been a dream? If so, she could not remember anything of it. She heard Sarah's voice far off, calling to Gwen. She would have liked to stay in bed, closing herself off from everyone, even Sarah. But she could not do that. Wearily she got out of bed.

She dragged herself through that day and spent another night in heavy dreamless sleep. The following morning Gwen and Sarah tried to persuade her to come down to Hugo's cottage with them, but she excused herself. She wandered aimlessly around the house for a time and then went into the hunting parlour: it had sporting prints on the walls and stuffed and mounted heads of foxes, their glassy eyes knowing and sly but amiable. There was also a piano, a Bechstein grand. It had not been looked after, probably not been tuned for ten years or more, and the whole keyboard was flat, but she played the Mozart piece on it that she had been doing at school the previous term. Aunt Marion came in while she was playing. She said,

"That's nice. Kitty, I have news for you."

"Yes, Aunt Marion?"

"The things Hugo took – they're safe. They will be back here in a day or two."

"You mean, Hugo's sending them back?"

She could scarcely imagine conscience overcoming him, but fear of being caught might. Aunt Marion shook her head.

"Not quite. But I spoke to Naidler, my solicitor, when it happened, and he's seen to everything. He's quite a young man, but very capable. You will be able to rely on him when the time comes. He knew, or found out, who the people were who might be approached by someone wanting to sell the miniatures, and asked them to notify him if that happened and make an excuse to hold the man. Hugo turned up at a place in Bond Street and Naidler got a taxi and arrived while they were still discussing prices. He made Hugo take him to where he had the rest of the things, at a flat he had borrowed in Bayswater, and collected them. Then, as I'd asked, he gave him a sharp dressing down and a warning, and sent him off."

"He's got the silver as well?"

"Yes. Fortunately Hugo tried to dispose of the miniatures first. The silver might have been more difficult to trace."

Katharine said, "I'm very glad, Aunt Marion."

The thin face was smiling. She would be delighted at the way it had worked out, and at her own cleverness in putting her solicitor on to it. She said,

"Now we can forget about the whole wretched business."

"Yes."

"You've been worrying about it too much, Kitty." She was chiding but gently. "You made a mistake, something anyone can do. We have to learn to live with mistakes, not brood. And since everything's been recovered, there's no harm done."

Katharine said, with difficulty, "It's not just a question of the paintings and silver. Though of course I'm glad you're getting them back."

"No," Aunt Marion said, "I suppose it isn't. You are thinking of your own part in it. But you must not be so harsh a judge. We don't like someone the less for being silly, or even for thinking untrue and unpleasant things about us. We all have to forgive each other. And ourselves."

"Yes."

"There's something else I'd like you to know. I said you will find Naidler a reliable person. You will meet him soon. I have asked him to come down at the beginning of next week."

Katharine nodded in silence. She realized Aunt Marion was well meaning – the extent of that was a bit overwhelming – but she would have liked her to go, to be left in peace.

Aunt Marion said, "I told you that I was planning to change my will. I think I should say that I spoke to your father on the telephone, just before they left for France. He was very firm that he does not wish to be included in any new disposition of the estate."

She looked up quickly. The news surprised and delighted her, but she realized it might not be tactful to show it. Aunt Marion went on,

"He added, though, that if I wished to make any bequest directly to his children, he would be very happy. It is that which I propose to arrange with Naidler."

She shook her head violently. "I don't want it, either, Aunt Marion."

"You have no choice, child, at least not at this point. It will be held in trust until you are twenty-one. You will then be free to dispose of it as you wish, but first you must receive it. You may find that by that time it means more to you. There are always good uses to which money can be put, and I think you may come to feel that your judgement on this is as good as another's and better than most. As I do. I do not spend much on myself but I have my charities. It is pleasant to be able to do things for them."

Katharine could imagine it: a hundred pounds for the

crippled children, two hundred for the incurables, fifty for the poor of the parish . . . My Lady Bountiful, doling out largess. It was horrible, she thought, a taking of credit where none really was due; but she could also see the fascination. Playing god in one's own small way – and even doing it anonymously there was the inner knowledge, the secret satisfaction. Even if one got rid of the money in one go – handing it over to the NSPCC, say – was that any better? You could not escape from it once it was yours.

Aunt Marion said, "I told you before: you are more mature than Gwen or Sarah and I can discuss such things with you. There is more to it than that, though. I have told your father that I will make provision for you all, but it will not be equal provision. The bulk will come to you."

Katharine protested, "But that's not fair!"

She meant not fair to Gwen and Sarah, but deeper in her mind she thought: not fair to me. If the burden had to fall it should fall equally. Aunt Marion said,

"There is no such thing as absolute fairness in life, and no possibility of it. It is not fair that Gwen has a more winning personality than you, and Sarah a more loving one. I am being hard, you see. They will both have quite enough. The money is well taken care of and my charities do not keep pace with its increase. I was brought up to the creed of conserving capital, and if you conserve it you multiply it. Wealth is a trust, to be passed on, where there is no overriding family claim, to the person of one's choice. I choose that it should come to you. This house as well. I hope you will live in it after I am gone. It has fallen sadly into disrepair. That is my fault. There is a laziness of the spirit which comes with age. One knows the best has gone and one cannot be bothered to preserve a second-best. But it is wrong to feel that. There are good things yet to be. In these few days you have made me realize that and I am grateful for it. You are fond of this house?"

"Yes. Very. But . . ."

"Then it will be yours to look after and restore. You will find that money will be useful for that. And now let's have an end to talking about money: such a dull subject. Play something for me. I do not know much about music but you have a pretty touch."

At the very beginning of their stay Katharine had been surprised by Aunt Marion's strength of character. Thinking over the events of the past few days she was even more impressed by her aunt's generosity. It had been shown towards Hugo in refusing to set the police on him and then, when he was caught, giving instructions for him to be let off. She was probably the one who had paid up for him over the bad cheques too. Her behaviour towards Katharine herself had brought the point home further. Not in this question of inheritance, but in the fact that there had been no reproaches over her part in the Hugo business. "We don't like someone the less for thinking untrue and unpleasant things about us." That had stung but had not been intended to sting. And was true, she felt, in her aunt's case, though she could not imagine it being true of anyone else she knew.

Her response to it all was not one of affection – she still did not know if she liked her aunt or not – but of trust. She felt a sense of security, and a need to give something in return. Obedience, at least. She could do as her aunt urged and put an end to her brooding, which in any case had been casting a pall over Gwen and Sarah. So she made a conscious and determined effort to snap out of it. That afternoon she went with the others to Hugo's cottage and organized a general clear-up. They also weeded the vegetable patch and picked whatever was ready: peas, a few strawberries, the beans which Ludmilla had not succeeded in devouring. She worked with energy and a slightly feverish exhilaration. Gwen and Sarah responded to this, which in turn made things easier. That night she needed no prompting towards sleep. She dreamt of the woman in grey. She awoke in the morning knowing she had done so, and felt happy even though she could not remember anything of the dream.

The weather had broken and it rained during the morning. They spent the time in the tower-room, reading, idling and playing a game with a pack of cards Gwen had found. It started as a limited form of canasta, but developed a separate and comical identity as they made new rules to overcome the limitations of only having one pack.

In the afternoon there was sunshine, though the belt of cloud across the blue suggested that it might not last. They went out into the woods, not with any purpose this time but just wandering. They made some finds. A golf ball, glimpsed first as a blob of white in the dark angle between the ground and a fallen tree, aroused speculation. They decided that Aunt Marion's father might have had his own course here at one time and were rewarded by finding a hole and a No 8 marker on what must once have been a green but was now a riot of Bishop's Weed.

They also found, or at least Sarah did, a clump of old apple trees, twisted and bent and choked with undergrowth but still bearing a few small apples. Some were even fairly ripe – Beauty of Bath, Katharine thought – and they picked and ate them. It was while they were occupied with this that a few heavy drops of rain fell and looking up they saw the sky overcast again and threatening. Within seconds it was raining fast.

They were a long way from the house. The trees afforded some shelter but not much. Gwen said,

"If this was an orchard there should have been a house or cottage near by. Probably a ruin but it would be better than nothing."

Sarah said, "I saw the wall just now. Over that way."

She pointed. Katharine and Gwen said, more or less together,

"The other lodge . . ."

They ran in the direction Sarah had indicated. They found the wall and then saw the gates and the lodge, less than fifty feet away. The rain had slackened a bit but the downpour was steady and the sky dark. Gwen reached the lodge first and heaved on the bolt outside the door. She panted and swore and said,

"I think it's rusted in. Oh, curse!"

Katharine said, "Let me have a try."

Gwen stepped aside and huddled up against the wall, trying to shelter from the rain. Katharine got hold of the bolt and pulled. It did not move. She braced a foot against the door jamb and tried again, using all her strength. With a squeal of metal it gave, just a little. She heaved once more and it budged distinctly. Gwen called, "Hurry up, Samson. I'm getting soaked." Katharine ignored the remark and took a new hold. The bolt came all the way out of its socket and she pushed open the door and went in.

There was enough light from the empty windows on the far side to see that the place was a ruin, the bare boards of the floor littered with rubbish, the walls naked except for a few trailing strips of paper and some roughly chalked phrases, either political or rude. But at least it offered protection from the rain. Gwen and Sarah followed her in. Gwen made a face, sniffing.

"Charming, isn't it? If the other place was anything like this, Hugo must have had a job clearing it up."

"It wouldn't be," Katharine said. "That cottage is isolated. People have done most of the damage here – kids from the housing estate, probably."

Sarah asked, "What was that?"

"What?"

"A noise. In the next room."

"I didn't hear anything," Gwen said. "What sort of noise?"

"Something moving."

"A rat," Gwen suggested, shuddering.

"No, bigger."

They stared at the door leading to the second room for a moment or two. Then Katharine said,

"We can always look."

She tried to say it casually but did not feel all that casual. The naked squalor of the cottage was depressing but also unnerving; and the beat and drip of rain did not help. She went to the door and pulled it open. It would not open fully because a pile of bricks prevented it, but she had a gap she could wriggle through.

The room was darker than the first, the unboarded window being partly blocked by an old cupboard with no door. There was altogether a great deal more junk here, including a rusting bed whose naked springs were covered with sheets of newspaper that clung to their sagging contour: someone had slept there. But there was no sign of anyone now. Sarah must have been wrong. Or perhaps whoever it was – one of the children from the housing estate maybe – had heard them talking and escaped through the window.

She went to look and had to go round the battered cupboard to do so. Then she stopped in shock and fear. He

131

was right in front of her, no more than inches away, crouching between cupboard and wall. She saw a man's staring face: black skin and gleaming white teeth, lips drawn in a frightening snarl of hatred.

8

Involuntarily Katharine flinched and stepped back. He spoke as she did so.

"Miss. Please, miss . . ."

The tone was not threatening but entreating. In the flood of relief she looked more closely at the face and saw how much she had misread the expression. It was not a snarl of hate but a grimace of fear. The skin was dark olive rather than black, the features Indian. And he was not a man, she realized, but a boy, slimly built, her own age or not much more.

She said, "Who are you? What are you doing here?"

He started to speak but stopped as Gwen squeezed through the door behind her, followed by Sarah. He looked still more alarmed; then, as he realized they were only girls, slightly relieved. He began to speak in a nervouse heavily accented voice. His name was Jamini Chundragar. He came from Pakistan, from Dacca. He was here because Joe had brought him. That was yesterday afternoon. Jo, had said someone called Charlie would come at night for him; but no one had come.

Gwen said, "But why should anyone bring you to a filthy ruin like this? And why stay here?"

"Because . . ."

He stopped, either because his English failed him or through reluctance. Katharine asked,

"How long have you been in England?"

He stared at her in silence. She thought he had not understood and repeated the question. He made a helpless shrugging gesture. In her mind things connected: his fear, hiding away behind the cupboard when she came into the room, the proximity of the Manpool docks. She said,

"You're an illegal immigrant – is that it? You haven't got a passport."

"I have passport," he said. "Pakistani passport. But not visa."

He seemed reconciled to telling them and the story came in a flood, only checked occasionally while he hunted for a word. His uncle had come to England several years before, when it was possible to enter freely. His father had died when he was small. His uncle had written that he was saving money to bring him and his mother to England. Then the law was changed and it was no longer possible. Last year his mother died. His uncle had managed to get money to him. A friend had told him of an English sailor who would help him to stow away on his ship, get him to England and his uncle. This is what had happened. The sailor had smuggled him ashore at Manpool and brought him here in a car. He could not take him all the way to where his uncle lived because he must not be long absent from the ship which was sailing again in a few hours. The man Charlie would take him the rest of the way.

Gwen said, "It doesn't look as though Charlie is going to turn up."

Jamini nodded. "I think not, also."

"If there is a Charlie. Where does he live, your uncle?"

"In Birmingham." He tapped the pocket of his thin blue jacket. "I have address."

"You can get a train from Manpool," Gwen said. "It's not all that far."

"I have no money," the boy said. "Joe took all that was left, for Charlie. He said it was necessary because there was risk. Charlie will be sent to prison if he is caught helping me."

"Holiday money," Gwen said. She looked at Katharine. "You're treasurer. Will it run to it?"

"Yes, but . . ."

"No buts."

"Even if he had money, he's got to find his way into Manpool again, find the station, buy a ticket – all that sort of thing. And he's in a completely foreign country. If he asks questions someone may report him to the police. That was the whole point of having this Charlie man take him."

Jamini nodded quickly. Gwen said,

"O.K., so one of us had better go with him."

"Look," Katharine said, "we need to think about this." She turned to the boy. "Will you stay here? We'll come back and help, but keep out of sight till we do. All right?"

He nodded again, more reluctantly. He had obviously been more impressed by Gwen's eagerness to help. Gwen said,

"He can't stay *here*, in this pigsty. We must take him up to the House at least."

"And run into the Captain on the way?" Katharine asked. "Remember that conversation a few days ago? Look, we'll come back. You do believe that, don't you?"

He said, "Yes", with some hesitation. Then more strongly, "I believe you."

They went back to the House along the drive. The rain had lessened but they were soon very wet. Katharine said,

"The obvious thing is to get Aunt Marion to help."

"If she will help."

"I'm sure she will."

"But if she won't?"

"Then we'll have to do it. But she will. Look at Hugo. She might get the Captain to take him to Birmingham by car. It's the safest way."

"After what he said about blacks? *You* reminded me of that."

"He'll do as Aunt Marion tells him."

If not out of pure devotion, she thought, under the threat of losing that legacy. Money did have some advantages.

"And who tells her?" Gwen asked. "All of us?"

"I don't think so. Better if one person does it."

"In that case it had better be you. You're the one she has the cosy chats with."

Katharine said, "Yes, I suppose so."

Sarah said, "Do you think we could ask Mrs Castle if she could make a curry for him?"

"Not a word to Mrs Castle. Even if she was all right you couldn't trust her not to talk to the Captain."

Gwen said, "I second that."

They entered the house without seeing anyone. From the kitchen they could hear Mrs Castle's radio booming something about unmarried mothers; she was devoted to "Woman's Hour". They parted for their different rooms. In hers, Katharine rubbed herself fairly dry and changed. She went downstairs again and along to Aunt Marion's sitting-room. She knocked and was told to come in.

Aunt Marion had the same programme on her radiogram with the funny knobs and old-fashioned dial. She was sitting in her chair by the window. She said,

"Hello, Kitty. You may switch the wireless off."

"If you're listening to something . . ."

"Only because I have tired my eyes reading, and the wireless is better than looking out of the window at the rain. Come and sit by me."

Katharine switched off the radio. She went to her aunt but did not sit down. She said,

"Actually, there is something important, Aunt Marion."

"What is it?"

"I've found someone, a boy, a Pakistani." She had been about to say 'We' but changed it to 'I' at the last moment, without knowing quite why she did so. "He wants to get to his uncle and I said I'd help him."

She saw the slight shadow on her aunt's face and suddenly there was a tight knot of nervousness in her stomach. Aunt Marion said,

"Why does he need help?"

"He has no money."

"And you want me to give you money for him?"

"No. It's not that."

"Then what?"

"He doesn't know how to get there and . . . he's frightened of being stopped by the police."

"You mean," Aunt Marion said, "he is a criminal?"

"No. No, he isn't."

"If he has done nothing wrong he has nothing to fear from the police."

"They would send him back, to Pakistan."

"I see." Aunt Marion paused. "He has come into the country illegally, then?"

She told her aunt most of the story they had had from Jamini though without mentioning where they had found him. The flicker of a frown at 'Pakistani' and an unresponsiveness in tone afterwards had made her wary. When the next question came she was ready to make her own challenge.

Aunt Marion asked. "Where is he now, this boy?"

Katharine said, "You are going to help him, aren't you?"

Again there was a silence before Aunt Marion said,

"The best way of helping him is to put him in the hands of the authorities."

"No." Katharine shook her head. "It's not. He wants to get to his uncle. He'll be all right then."

"He has broken the law," Aunt Marion said. "I can understand your being sympathetic, especially if he is an orphan as he claims, but that is the crux of the matter. And anyone who helps him to avoid being caught would also be breaking the law. You must tell me where he is hiding, Kitty."

"No," Katharine said. "I'm sorry."

Her throat felt dry and she was afraid her legs would tremble. She turned and started to walk towards the door. Aunt Marion called,

"Stop. Come back here." She stopped and turned but did not go towards her. "Where were you going?"

"Out."

"You were going to help this boy." Katharine did not reply. "I forbid it. Do you hear me?"

"Yes."

"Listen. The law is something very important, possibly the most important thing there is. Without law, everything falls apart. It is a duty on all of us to support it, and to support the police in enforcing it."

Katharine said, "Hugo broke the law."

"The offence he committed was against me. He could not be accused of anything unless I brought charges. And I did not choose to, because of his mother."

"He did wrong. He lied and cheated and stole. Jamini's not done any of those things. In fact, he's been lied to and cheated and stolen from. The sailor took the last bit of his money and abandoned him."

"All that happened because *he* cheated in the first place. He knew he had no right to enter this country. He also knows that if he can evade the police for six months he will be safe and can stay. It must not be allowed to happen."

"Why? Does it matter? One boy, coming to live in England?"

"It matters," Aunt Marion said. "Even if it did not, there would still be one's duty to the law. But it matters. It matters a great deal that these people, who are not English in any way, who have their own habits and customs quite different from ours, are coming here, flooding in, taking over our cities. They are changing England, whose strength was that she did not change. I disapproved of the Rhodesians rebelling against the Queen. That does not mean I want black faces all round me, their sing-song voices in my ears. I love this country. I would hate to see it ruined by these . . . creatures."

She had spoken with increasing bitterness. Katharine said,

"One boy."

"Where one succeeds in getting through, others follow. The law and the principle must be upheld."

They faced each other in silence. Katharine saw the thin bloodless lips in the old face pursed in anger. She herself felt exhausted and unhappy. She said,

"May I go, Aunt Marion?"

"When you have told me where the boy is hiding."

"So that you can get the police? I won't tell you."

"I insist." Katharine made no reply. "Then you will go at once to your room, and stay there until you are

139

prepared to behave in a proper manner." Katharine nodded and started towards the door. "Wait."

"Yes, Aunt Marion."

"Mrs Castle will take you."

She pulled the tattered silk rope which would set the bell jangling in the kitchen and drop the red flash into its appropriate box. Nothing was said during the minute that passed before Mrs Castle's footsteps were heard and she knocked and entered. Aunt Marion said,

"Miss Katharine is to go to her room, Castle. Kindly escort her. Then lock the door and keep the key safe."

Mrs Castle looked startled but said,

"Yes, ma'am."

Katharine walked ahead of her along the corridor and upstairs. When they were out of range of the sitting-room, Mrs Castle said,

"What's all this over, then?"

"Nothing much."

"It don't look like nothing much! Well, if you want to keep it to yourself I'm sure it's all the same to me."

They reached the bedroom and Katharine went in. Mrs Castle took the key from inside the door. She said,

"Whatever it is, you're a fool to be upsetting your aunt. She's an easy enough woman except when she's crossed. Then watch out. If I was you, young lady, I'd think very serious before I set myself up to defy her. Very serious indeed."

She closed the door and locked it and her footsteps went away along the corridor.

Gwen whispered through the door,

"Kate! You there?"

"Where else?" She swung her legs off the bed and went to the door. "Sorry I can't ask you in."

Gwen giggled nervously. "No. What happened, Kate?"

"What have you been told?"

"Only by Mrs Castle – that you're to be locked in your room till further orders. She was frantically curious why."

Katharine said sharply, "You didn't tell her anything?"

"No fear."

"Nor Sarah?"

"We both looked astonished. Sarah put it on very well. I didn't know she could act like that."

"Where is Sarah?"

"Top of the stairs, keeping watch."

She said approvingly, "Good."

"But what *happened*? I mean – locking you in your room! Like something from Dickens. What made her go berserk?"

Katharine told her. Gwen said,

"She was really wild about it?"

"Wild enough."

"Are you going to . . .?"

"What?"

"Tell her where he is."

"No."

She spoke curtly, angry at Gwen for suggesting it, and at herself because of the fear that rose when she repeated her defiance in front of a third person. She could only guess what she might be letting herself in for. Gwen asked,

"How long do you think she'll keep you here?"

"Long enough." It was some relief to concentrate on the immediate problem. "Look, we've got to work things out about getting Jamini away."

"Well, I'd better, hadn't I, since you can't? You've got the money. You could push it under the door . . ."

"No, I'm going to do it."

"How?" Gwen asked. "By jumping out of the

window?" The tone was presumably sarcastic, but the door muffled it to blankness. "There's a twenty-foot drop and it's a cobbled walk."

"*Neither* of us could do anything right now. Too much chance of being seen and followed. It will have to wait till night – or early morning, rather. And before then you can find where Mrs Castle puts the key to this room. She's bound to come up some time, with bread and water if nothing else, and you can watch her. I want you to get it for me tonight, after she's gone to bed. And it would be a good idea to bring me that alarm clock from the kitchen, because I'll need to wake up early – and food: Jamini's probably hungry already and he'll be ravenous by then."

"Do you think he'll stay here? He'll be expecting us back sooner."

"I think he'll stay. He's pretty scared."

Gwen said, "I still don't see why I couldn't go and get him away. Or we could both go."

"That would be silly. There's no point in two of us getting involved. And anyway I'll need you to cover up here. We'll talk about that later."

"All right."

It was said reluctantly but Gwen was yielding fairly easily, Katharine realized. She thought of some of the difficulties ahead of her and suppressed another urge towards panic. She said,

"Aunt Marion will probably question you, to see if you know anything. Sarah, too, maybe, but I should think mostly you."

"That's easy. I can lie better than you can."

It was true. Katharine said,

"She'll want to know why you weren't with me when I found him."

"Nothing in it. You disappeared in one of your moods.

142

Very convincing, in view of the way you've been behaving lately."

Also true. Katharine said,

"You'd better go now. They may be looking for you. And make sure you're not seen when you come back."

"Trust me."

Her footsteps went away and Katharine lay down again on the bed. Silence lay heavy on the house. The rain had stopped and the only sound was the screech of a jay, muted and flattened by distance. She was very conscious of being alone.

The slowness of time passing rasped her nerves. She had some books which she had brought to read at night but she could not settle to any of them. Words danced incomprehensibly before her eyes, and she was irritated to find, over and over again, that she had read several pages without any meaning coming through, and with no more than a minute or two elapsed of the agonizing crawl of the hands round the dial of her watch. She tried alternately to think and not to think about what she was planning to do. It was hard to say which was more depressing.

Once again the only thing that brought any ease was remembering the woman in grey. She tried to build up a picture of her, of what her life had been like. Had she married and had children? For some reason she did not think so. Most of her life spent here in this house, she had said: in a dream, of course, but the dream was still as real and important as the recollection of her aunt's tight angry face an hour ago. Would the woman in grey have approved her action? She was deeply and irrationally sure she would. The thought helped.

Mrs Castle came just after six. She unlocked the door, struggling with it for some moments and muttering under her breath, and set a tray down on the bedside table. There was cold beef, bread and butter, a slice of cake and a cup of cocoa. Mrs Castle said,

"There. That's to do you till breakfast."

Katharine said, "Thank you."

"I can't understand you, doing a thing like that. I'd thought you were such a sensible girl." She paused but Katharine did not answer. "Upsetting your aunt, your own flesh and blood, on account of one of those foreign blacks. And your aunt in poor health, too."

She had clearly been told the whole story. Katharine said,

"I didn't mean to upset her."

"You ought to have known it would, someone as bright as you." There was no useful comment to this and Katharine again kept silent. "She's very upset indeed. If you'd come to me instead I'd have told you what she'd be like. I know how things take her."

"Would you have helped me," Katharine asked, "to help the Pakistani boy?"

"I might."

She had an impulse to say: then do it now – to tell her where Jamini was and what needed to be done to get him away. It would be such a relief to rid herself of the load. Mrs Castle repeated, "I might," looking closely at her, and Katharine steadied herself. She remembered what Hugo had told her of the expectations Mrs Castle and the Captain had.

Mrs Castle said, "She said just bread and meat, but I put a slice of cake on as well. I don't like to see you locked up like this."

That was probably true; and it was probably true that, other things being equal, she would have helped Jamini. She was not a bad woman at heart and not rigid about things like Aunt Marion. But she certainly would not risk losing the security of her old age for a coloured boy from a faraway land. She could not, Katharine thought, her mind once more tired and dull, be expected to. She said,

"Thank you, Mrs Castle. I'm all right, really."

"You should think again. It's a bad business." She paused. "And it could be a costly one."

The warning this time was naked. Katharine turned her head away. Mrs Castle said,

"My dear, I do wish you wouldn't be silly. I do wish it."

Gwen came up with the key and the other things late at night, when the house was quiet. Katharine rehearsed her in the events of the following morning. Her own absence was unlikely to be discovered until breakfast at nine o'clock. The household was not an early rising one – the Captain was the only one who got up before eight and he went out after making himself a cup of tea in the kitchen. She *might* be able to see Jamini on to his train and get back by then, in which case, with a little luck in getting into her room and the door relocked, they might not even know she had been away.

But they had to face the possibility of things not working out as perfectly as that. If Mrs Castle or Aunt Marion did find that Katharine was missing, Gwen would be the obvious suspect to have helped her. The only thing then would be to admit it – to say Katharine had asked her to get the key and she had done so. She could also say that Katharine had told her she was slipping out to warn Jamini to get clear. She was not to admit any more but, if pressed, could say she had an idea that Katharine might have gone to Hugo's cottage the previous afternoon. That might send Aunt Marion – or more likely the Captain – on a chase in the wrong direction.

Katharine set the alarm for half past five. She slept well and woke on the first ring, immediately stopping the bell which sounded shatteringly loud in the dawn. She jumped out of bed and dressed quickly. Now that she was actually doing something the fears had gone and she felt confident.

To make sure her absence went unnoticed as long as possible, she replaced the key to her room on the nail from which Gwen had said she'd taken it and got out of the house through a window, carefully pulling it to after her. She kept close in to the side of the house and when she had to break cover ran like mad. The sky was clear and deep blue overhead but cloudy red behind her, the sun up but hidden. She heard a bird high and far off, a lark probably, and saw rabbits bounding away on either side: a dozen or more. Then she was in the shelter of the woods and could walk.

Her enthusiasm was reduced a bit by the sight of the gatehouse with its forbidding boarded windows. She went to the door which they had left unbolted – a stupid thing to do, she realized, because the Captain might have noticed it when opening or closing the gates. She pushed it open and called,

"Jamini! Are you all right?"

He answered indistinctly. She heard him moving in the other room and he came through. She saw he was shivering. He said,

"I thought you will not come."

"I'm here. I've brought some food. Eat it."

He took the package and opened it. Inside were cheese sandwiches which Gwen had made. He started eating eagerly, then stopped.

"You, miss? Do you not eat?"

"I'm all right. And not miss. Call me Katharine. Kate, if you find it easier."

146

"I cannot tell how grateful I am."

"Listen," she said. "You will have to get to Birmingham by train. That means first getting to the railway station in Manpool. I'm going to go with you and buy the ticket."

"I have no money."

"I know. It doesn't matter. I've got enough for it."

"My uncle will pay you back. I promise most solemnly that . . ."

He had stopped eating. She said,

"I don't want to rush you, but the sooner we're away from here the better."

He nodded, and bolted the sandwiches. When he had finished they climbed through the broken window into the waste land beyond the wall. She looked carefully before they started to cross it but there was no sign of life from the distant houses. She said,

"This is the risky part. Get ready to run and keep close behind me."

She heard him panting heavily at her heels. He was not in very good condition but physically altogether he looked weak and undernourished. She slowed again once they were among the houses. They were still conspicuous but less so walking than running. She kept a sharp eye on the houses as they passed. She heard a radio playing loudly from inside one but the curtains were drawn and she saw no one.

Another ten minutes brought them to the main road. There was no sign of traffic and she decided to walk on in the direction of Manpool. There was a stretch farther along with no houses, where she felt waiting would be safer.

Jamini asked, "We await a bus?"

"No. I'm not sure they run on this road and anyway

not at this time of day. We'll have to rely on getting a hitch." He looked blank. "A lift from a car driver."

He nodded in acquiescence. At least he seemed prepared to leave everything to her, without argument. They stood by the roadside. A couple of lorries came but travelling from Manpool; nothing the other way. The waiting began to get on her nerves. Jamini on the other hand seemed quite relaxed. He hummed a weird tune which irritated her after a time. Her stomach was reminding her that she had not had anything since early the previous evening.

A car going the right way came at last but the driver ignored them. It seemed a long time before another appeared. It was a new saloon car, a man driving. She thumbed and it rolled to a halt beside them. The man wound the window down. He asked her,

"Where you aiming for?"

"Manpool. George Street station. Can you . . .?"

He was large and blond, about fifty, with watery eyes that had been examining them closely. He said,

"What is this, anyway?" He gave a chuckling laugh. "An elopement?"

She felt herself flushing. "It's just that we have a train to catch. We'd be very greateful if you could give us a lift."

The watery eyes turned on her. He said,

"Room for you, if you like. But Pakki Pete will have to run behind."

Katharine turned away, not answering. The man said,

"I don't know who your parents are, but they ought to look after you better. Makes you sick. No wonder this country's in the mess it's in. People letting kids carry on any way they like."

She still did not answer. It was a relief when, with a parting volley of filthy abuse, he drove away. Jamini said,

"I am sorry."

She said bitterly, "You don't need to be. It's not your fault."

"If you leave me here I will be all right maybe."

"You just do as I say!"

She spoke more sharply than she had intended. He nodded and they stood in silence. A car and a truck passed but the drivers ignored her signals. Five minutes later a lorry picked them up.

They sat in the cab with the driver. He was amiable but curious: what were they doing on the road at this time of day? Katharine had had time to invent a story since the incident with the man in the saloon car, and she told it as glibly as she could. They were on an initiative test as part of the programme for a Duke of Edinburgh Award.

She relied on the lorry driver knowing even less about the Awards scheme than she did. He nodded and said, looking across her at Jamini,

"'Im, too?"

"My brother? Yes. We're both doing it."

"Your *brother*? Come off it!"

"Adopted. I have another, from Vietnam, and a Chinese sister. There was a programme about us on television."

"Oh, yes?"

"Did you see it?" she asked.

"I don't see much telly, what with bein' on the road most of the time. I think I remember the wife sayin' somethin' about it, though."

It was not all that difficult to get away with lying, she thought. Just make it a real staggerer, and throw in the Royal Family and television. The driver was obviously delighted with them, and with the story he could take back to his wife. He went out of his way to drop them at the railway station.

.   .   .   .   .

149

It was almost eight o'clock and the next train to Birmingham did not leave until eight-fifty. So much, she thought, for her hopes of getting back before she'd been missed. Katharine got cups of British Rail tea for both of them – Jamini smelled it with surprise and sipped it with a wondering air – and then they sat on an out-of-the-way seat until it was time to get him aboard. She found him an empty compartment and gave him his ticket. At Birmingham, she told him, he must get a taxi and give the driver the paper with his uncle's address. The money she was able to give him after buying the ticket might not be enough, but his uncle could pay when the taxi got there.

"On the other side of the paper, will you write me the address of your house?"

"Haven't a pencil. Why, anyway?"

"So that my uncle can send back the money."

"There's no need, Jamini."

He said earnestly, "But he will wish to do so."

"No. A letter would not be safe. Someone might open it and trace you."

"You will not be in trouble because of this helping me?"

"No. But it's better to take no chances."

"I shall not see you again?"

"Probably not. Who knows, though?"

"All my life I will remember your kindness."

Now that she had achieved her objective she felt depressed. Jamini had a sore at the corner of his mouth and he did not smell very pleasant, though that was scarcely surprising after the way he'd had to live recently. She had discovered also that he had an offputting habit of sniffing loudly at uncertain intervals. Behind him she saw a furious Aunt Marion, and retribution which was unguessable but likely to be dire. She wished the train would go.

"All my life," he repeated, putting a hand out of the window to grasp hers tightly. "Katharine . . ."

He sniffed loudly. She said,

"I hope you'll be happy in England, Jamini."

The train started at last. He waved until the bend in the track carried him away. It was five to nine by the station clock as she walked along the platform. She had better start finding her way back. There was no point in delaying it.

9

Aunt Marion said, "Where is the boy?"

"I don't know."

"You are lying. If you had only gone out to warn him you would have been back long before this. You have taken him somewhere. I insist that you tell me."

Katharine said, half-truthfully, thinking of the long miles between Manpool and Birmingham,

"I don't know where he is."

"But you know where he is going?"

She swallowed her scruples. "No."

They were in Aunt Marion's sitting-room, to which Katharine had been taken by a grim-faced Captain Benger who had spotted her coming up the drive. Aunt Marion sat in her high-backed chair and Katharine faced her. The Captain stood by the door. Katharine felt tired and a bit hysterical. Was he there to prevent her making a dash for it, or to protect Aunt Marion in case she took the brass poker from beside the firedog and attacked her?

"I have been mistaken in you," Aunt Marion said, "very much mistaken. I see that what I took for strength of character is really wilfulness and obstinacy. I placed a trust in you, now and for the future. You have betrayed it."

She would rather have stayed silent but could not help saying,

"No."

"I say you have. And it is a trust that can never be restored. Never."

She said nothing to that. The meaning was fairly clear. No house, no fortune, for wicked Katharine. She felt light-headed. Pop goes the heiress . . . And miserable. Not for the fortune; but it was hard to say goodbye, even after so short a time, to the hope of living here some day.

Aunt Marion said, "But regardless of that, I will *not* be defied. I will find out where this coloured boy is and have him handed over to the authorities. If you are sensible you will help me voluntarily."

And if not, what? Whippings, thumbscrews – the gallows? She looked past her aunt without speaking. Aunt Marion went on,

"It will be humiliating to report you yourself to the police, but I shall do so if there is no alternative. The disgrace, to me and to your family, matters less than permitting you to act in this way, flouting all decency and discipline."

She must be joking, Katharine thought; but she looked at her and saw that she was not. The thin face was sharp and white. She thought about the possibility of her having another heart attack and felt sick. Aunt Marion said,

"Tell me where he is, Katharine."

Whatever happened, she could not do that. She said, "I'm sorry, Aunt Marion."

Her aunt said, "I hope you will be." Her tone was hard and bitter. "I shall give you an hour to think about it. At the end of that time, if you are still unreasonable, I shall ring the police and ask them to send someone to make a full investigation. I shall also telephone your parents in France and tell them I refuse to be responsible for you any longer. This will mean, of course, that they must end their holiday and come back."

She stared at Katharine, waiting. When there was no reply, she said,

"Captain, will you please take her away. Not to her own room. I want no further communication between them before the police arrive. Put her in the tower wing."

The heavy door slammed behind her and she heard the key turn rustily in the lock. She had a sick empty feeling. It was partly ordinary hunger, probably, but it came more from misery and despair. Her aunt, she knew, would not budge. There would be police and questionings.

She was not any longer worried about the consequences for herself. Or her parents. It would be a pity about their holiday being ruined, but there were much worse things that could happen. Such as Jamini being arrested and sent back to a country where he had no one. The irritation she had felt at the station no longer mattered. What counted was that he was on his own and in need of help. She could not betray him, whatever threats were made.

But she realized also that her defiance in the end made no difference: he would be found. Gwen knew about the train to Birmingham and so did Sarah. It was unlikely that Gwen would hold out against questions put by a police officer, impossible that Sarah should. She would be in tears before they started and sobbing out everything within a couple of minutes.

After that, it was all too easy. They would telephone the Birmingham police and have men waiting at the ticket barrier. They could not possibly miss him. Even if the train had got in before they arrived, they would only have to ask among the taxi men and find who had picked him up and to what address he had been taken.

It would have been a relief to cry but her eyes were hot and dry. Her head ached with frustration and despair. It was the helplessness which was worst: her own and Jamini's, with everything moving inescapably towards their defeat, and his capture. If there were anything she could do, anything she could give to save him, it would not be so bad. The house – much as she loved it, she renounced that willingly, gladly. If there were something else . . . But there was nothing. No chance, no hope.

Then she saw her. It started as it had done before with a sense of silence, wrapping her round, almost tangible. Her eyes were drawn to the spiral staircase. The woman in grey stood near the top, looking down. Katharine could see the carved wood of the staircase behind her, and yet could see her clearly.

She moved forward into the zone of silence. At the foot of the stairs she stopped. She said, her voice sounding thin and echoing,

"Is there any way of helping? Please tell me."

The woman did not speak but nodded slightly. Katharine tried to read her expression. It was a look of acceptance: of knowing that bad things must happen – shame, despair, pain. But not of unhappiness, because there was something else as well. A serenity at having got through the miseries, overcome them, turned them, even, to good account.

She asked, "Shall I come up?"

The figure nodded again. She felt fear now, not of the woman but of what was going to happen. She did not know what it was except that it would be bad, very bad. And yet necessary.

She began to climb the stairs. There were the usual creaks and protests from the wood. The figure faded as she approached her but that did not matter. She felt at peace.

The fear had gone, and when the wood of the staircase groaned on a different note, sharper, harsher, suddenly yielding, and swayed and cracked under her feet, the fear did not come back.

She was pinned under a rubble of wood and plaster: half the ceiling seemed to have come down on her as well. One leg was sickeningly twisted and hurting dreadfully. The noise, sounding as though the whole house were collapsing, had subsided but dust hung in the air. She thought someone must have heard and would come, but minutes went by and no one did. The sound would have been muffled by the tower's thick walls, and anyway there was the conservatory between this and the main part of the house.

She said, gasping from the dust:

"Help me . . ."

The woman in grey knelt beside her. Now she was no shadowy wraith, but substantial, real as she had been in the dream.

Katharine said: "It hurts . . ."

"I know." A hand grasped hers. "Hold on."

The pain did not go but she found she could bear it better. She said:

"You knew . . . that this would happen."

"Yes."

She looked into brown eyes that were strangely familiar, a face she almost recognized.

"I don't understand."

The hand pressed hers. "You will."

She thought of her despair of a few minutes earlier, of Jamini and her desperate need to help him. She had a certainty that her pain and helplessness were linked with that. She asked:

"Has it been paid for now?"

"Yes. Paid for."

She said suddenly: "I know who you are!"

The woman smiled. "Then rest."

The pain went, everything went, into a golden mist. She was unconscious when the Captain came to unlock the door.

Her father said: "Well, lass, how's everything? Fortunately not as bad as it looks, the doctors tell me."

Her right leg, encased in plaster, was suspended over the hospital bed by an arrangement of pulleys and wires. Katharine said:

"Hello, Daddy." He stooped to kiss her. "I'm all right, really. They didn't have to drag you back."

"No trouble at all. Your mother will be along in a few minutes. She got called to the telephone the moment she got here – one of her delinquent girls in trouble, I gather."

She nodded. "Have you seen Aunt Marion?"

"Briefly. She's very upset about this."

"I know."

"She feels it's all her fault. She was warned years ago there was rot in that part of the house, but she put off doing anything about it. She's set in her ways, and it would have been a nuisance, having workmen in. She's bitterly sorry about it now, of course. She blames herself so much, I don't think it would help for us to add to it."

"No."

"In fact . . . You're going to need a fairly long convalescence – it will cut into next term, I'm afraid. She'd like you to spend some of the time with her. If you don't mind . . . I think it might be a good thing. Help her not to accuse herself so much; and, as I say, she's an old woman."

What was unsaid came over more clearly than his actual

words: an old woman, and rich. But it was no longer important. She nodded.

"Of course I'll go."

"She's very fond of you, you know."

"Yes, I know."

"But first they've got to finish patching you up here."

"My leg's pretty bad, isn't it?"

He patted her hand, smiling reassuringly. "Nothing that a good doctor can't put right."

"But even when they've finished, I'll walk with a limp."

"No. Of course you won't." He spoke too hastily. "Whatever gave you a silly idea like that?"

He was thinking, she realized, that she must have overheard something said by one of the nurses or doctors. She could scarcely tell him the truth: that she had seen a figure in grey, a ghost not of some stranger from the past but of her own future self.

She smiled, to reassure him in turn.

"It doesn't matter. Honestly."